Charlotte Elizabeth Bowen, Frederick Gilbert

Christian Hatherley's childhood

Charlotte Elizabeth Bowen, Frederick Gilbert

Christian Hatherley's childhood

ISBN/EAN: 9783337024888

Printed in Europe, USA, Canada, Australia, Japan

Cover: Foto ©Andreas Hilbeck / pixelio.de

More available books at **www.hansebooks.com**

'I have to lie on this sofa week after week,
month after month.' *Page* 12.

CHRISTIAN HATHERLEY'S CHILDHOOD.

A Tale.

By C. E. B.,

AUTHOR OF "WORK FOR ALL," "RICH AND POOR,"
ETC. ETC.

WITH FOUR ILLUSTRATIONS.

SEELEY, JACKSON, AND HALLIDAY, 54, FLEET STREET,
LONDON. MDCCCLXXII.

CHRISTIAN HATHERLEY'S CHILDHOOD.

CHAPTER I.

> " 'Twas but the child of poverty,
> Born to no wealth or fame;
> And yet to one so weak and small
> They gave a noble name!"

THERE was sorrow of the saddest kind in the hitherto happy, though humble, abode of Lucy Hatherley. Her husband had been killed after they had been married but one year. He was a carpenter, living near London. The shock was too great for the poor young wife, who lay hovering between life and death, having just given birth to her first infant, a little girl.

"The child should be baptized," said the doctor; "it is scarcely likely to live."

The clergyman came. The little fragile, tender being lay in his arms.

"Name this child," said he.

It had not been thought of in the hurry. A neighbour stooped to its mother's pillow. Her eyes were open, and she was watching all that passed.

"What shall it be called?" asked the woman; "shall it be Lucy, after you?"

The dying woman shook her head. "Let it be 'Christian,'" said she; "it was my mother's name, and she was a good and holy woman."

So the babe was called "Christian," and then, at its mother's request, it was laid by her side for a few minutes, whilst she gazed tenderly on its features.

"If she dies, well," said she. "If she lives, may she be a Christian in deed as well as name, for she will be left alone in the world. May God bless my babe."

Then the mother died, but the infant throve and grew strong.

There were no very near relations to take charge of the orphan, and it would have been carried to the workhouse had not a cousin of the father's come forward. Miss Bonar was a dressmaker, who rather prided herself on her gentility; she could not endure the idea of a relation of hers going on the parish as a pauper. Such a thing had never been heard of in their family, she said; so to prevent the disgrace, she arranged with a respectable woman near Kensington, where she herself resided, to bring up the child.

Fortunately little Christian fell into kind hands, for Miss Bonar, thinking she had done as much as was necessary in agreeing to pay a weekly sum to Mrs. Gibson, did not trouble herself much farther; and had the child been neglected, she probably would have known little about it. But she was, on the contrary, as carefully tended as any of Mrs. Gibson's own children, and almost as dearly loved.

The Gibsons kept a shop, and were in a very small way, when Miss Bonar first placed her little relation in their charge. They gradually improved in their circumstances, and an unexpected legacy made them more than comfortable. The small sum paid for her foster-child was of no great consequence to Mrs. Gibson, but she would not have parted with her for this reason. Christian had a very happy childhood—plenty of love, plenty of brothers and sisters in the children of the family she lived with, and in consequence plenty of fun. She went to school as she grew older, for though her aunt, as she was taught to call Miss Bonar, did not like the additional expense, Mrs. Gibson almost insisted on her having the same simple educational advantages as her own children; and she had the more influence, because Miss Bonar was perfectly aware that the sum she paid the Gibsons was extremely small, and she had no desire to take a young child to live with herself. That she must come to her some day she was aware was probable, but this was for future consideration.

Thus Christian's early childhood passed almost without her knowing Miss Bonar; and as she was not a person to be attractive to a child when they did meet, she thought very little about her.

But a great trial was approaching. The clear sky of Christian's happiness was becoming overcast by a most unexpected cloud. When she was between eleven and twelve years old, the Gibsons came to the resolution of leaving their native country, and settling in Australia. A brother of Mrs. Gibson's was doing well there with his family, and wrote such urgent letters to them to go and follow his example, that, knowing him to be a man of sense and caution, they ventured to decide on following his advice, having several boys to put out in life. But their new plans necessarily involved leaving Christian behind them, —the gentle, loving girl so dear to them all. She was of a peculiarly unselfish, clinging nature, and so truthful and obedient, that Mrs. Gibson used to say she was just the right sort of child for her name. She had heard the particulars of that baptism from the woman who had nursed her mother, and from whose hands she had received the little orphan.

Mrs. Gibson would gladly have taken her with them, but her husband did not think it would be right to separate her from Miss Bonar, who was quite able to provide comfortably for her well-doing, being a lone woman, with no one else to care for; and Mrs. Gibson was obliged to own that she believed he was right.

Poor Christian was for a time perfectly inconsolable, when she found that the whole family was going away to leave her in England alone, for alone it appeared to her, so little did she know of the aunt, whose house was to become her future home.

Miss Bonar felt thankful this change of affairs had not taken place when Christian was younger. She intended to begin at once and teach her dressmaking, as she could already sew very neatly.

The dreaded day of separation came only too quickly. The child clung to her adopted mother in an agony of grief, declaring she should never be happy again, and that she could not bear to go and live with Miss Bonar.

Mrs. Gibson was a good woman in her way, and a wise one. She was anxious to brace the child's mind by making her feel it was her duty to bear well what could not be otherwise ordered.

" Cheer up, dear, cheer up," said she, " and try to submit to God's will. He ' tempers the wind to the shorn lamb,' and He will make you happy in your new home after a bit."

Still the child sobbed bitterly, and would not be comforted.

" Shall I tell you why your mother gave you your name ?" she continued. " She wished it to be ' Christian,' because she said it was her mother's name, who was a good woman ; and she hoped you would be a Christian in deed as well as in name, and

then all would be well with you. So you must try
and bear this trouble like one, dear."

The words were not without their effect afterwards, though they had apparently little at the
moment. The parting moment arrived, and Christian
never saw her friends again during the years of her
youth.

CHAPTER II.

"Yes, every day the Christian child
    His own especial cross must take ;
And even in the smallest things
    Must often fight for Jesus' sake.

" For if he stay the angry blow,
    Or if he check the hasty word,
And only gentle answers give,
    He fights a battle for the Lord."

MISS BONAR lived in a very small house, in a retired street. She kept one little maid of all work. She was not dependent on her dressmaking, but was fond of it, and worked constantly, and she intended that Christian should do the same.

Her first afternoon and evening in her new home were far from pleasant to a child who had been accustomed to the sociability and brightness of a cheerful family. Her aunt seldom saw any one, and rarely talked unless to find fault. Christian thought the hours would never pass till bed-time, and then she sobbed herself to sleep. The next day and all the after days were no better. She had to sit hour after hour hemming and stitching, till both head and heart ached as she thought over past days, and she wondered how she could ever endure those that were before her, with no one to love, and no one to love her—nothing to do but to run up long seams. Tears often blinded her eyes, and when her aunt saw it she grew angry with her; she was not in the habit of sympathizing with others. So Christian dried them, and tried to look cheerful, but her thoughts wandered to her lost foster-mother and the brothers and sisters who were now sailing away on the wide ocean which Christian had never so much as seen.

Miss Bonar was not altogether a bad-hearted woman, but she had never been accustomed to children, and she looked on Christian as a charge from which, being her only relation, she could not escape. She had lived a lonely and selfish life, caring for no one but herself; anxious to save money, and for that purpose labouring from morning to night much harder than she need have done, for, as we before remarked, she was not dependent on her dressmaking altogether. Her temper was so irritable, that she led her little maid of all work a sad time of it. She never had been able to keep one for long together on this account.

It was a dull, sad life, and Christian grew pale and silent; and even Miss Bonar began to think she would be better for more exercise, and sent her out oftener on messages and to take walks.

One day she told her to carry home a finished dress to a lady who lived at some little distance, charging her to wait and see if there were any message to bring back. She found the house, and was told to stay in the hall whilst the servant took the parcel to her mistress. After a time she was desired to go upstairs to receive some directions for Miss Bonar about the work.

She was shown into an elegant boudoir, where, on the sofa, lay a very sweet and young-looking lady, who appeared to be in delicate health.

She seemed to expect to see an older person enter, and said, in a gentle tone—

"I wanted to send a message to Miss Bonar about my dress, but I am afraid you are too young to understand it, my little girl; I had better write a note."

"I think I can explain anything, ma'am, if you will try me, ma'am. I live with Miss Bonar, and often take messages."

"Are you apprenticed to her?" asked Mrs. Clair, looking with much interest on little Christian, whose calm, thoughtful countenance struck her as unusual in a child.

"No, ma'am, I am a relation. I call her aunt, and I live with her now."

"Have you no parents?"

"No, they are dead, and my other parents are gone to Australia," and the child's lips trembled as she said this, for her heart and eyes filled whenever she spoke of the Gibsons.

"What do you mean by your other parents?" said Mrs. Clair, kindly; "tell me all about yourself."

Her gentle tone of voice and sweet countenance were not easy to resist. Christian soon found herself telling Mrs. Clair all she knew of her own history; of her love for the simple, warm-hearted family with whom she had been brought up, and of the weary, lonely life she led now.

"And so your mother wished you to be named Christian, and hoped you would be one in deed. Do you know what it means to be really a Christian, little girl?"

The child did not reply, and the lady continued—

"A Christian must try to be like Christ, you know; and He was gentle and obedient, and did God's will in all things. A Christian must not murmur over his or her lot, even if it is not a happy one. I find it hard work often not to complain of mine."

Christian opened her eyes with surprise at such a remark from one who seemed to have everything in the world to make her happy. The lady noticed it and said—

"I have to lie on this sofa week after week, month after month. I could walk about as well as you do a year ago. Then I was thrown from my horse, and my back was so hurt that the doctors keep me here, and they say it may be very long before I am well, if I ever shall be again. At first I thought I could never endure it, but then I remembered God would not give me more to bear than He saw I needed, and I can trust Him for the future. So must you, Christian. Try and be patient, and to believe that God loves you dearly, although He has taken your friends from you, and after a time you will be happy again."

"And now," said Mrs. Clair, "I must not keep you any longer, but I should like to see you sometimes. Your aunt often does work for me, so perhaps she will let you come whenever there is anything to send home, and remember, little Christian, to try and be worthy of your name."

Oh, how much can be effected by a few kind words! Christian had walked soberly and without spirit as she came. She skipped and ran as she returned, so light-hearted did she feel; and all because of the lady's kind sympathy with troubles which she could not remove.

Her aunt was more than usually cross that evening. Christian had given Mrs. Clair's message about the work clearly, but Miss Bonar was not pleased that any alteration was needful, and vented her ill-humour on the poor child.

Everything she did was wrong. If the scissors were lost, it was Christian who had them last, she was sure, and she was the most careless girl living; she was for ever losing something or other. When at length they were found in her own work-bag, she insinuated that they had been slipped in on the sly. When she told her to thread her needle for her, she declared that she was as long as possible about it, because she knew she was in a hurry. And she gave

her such a long task of work to do, that the child
could scarcely keep her eyes open till it was finished.
On some evenings Miss Bonar would have let her put
it away, and go to bed, but not only was every stitch
to be done, but, when finished, she insisted on part
of it being unpicked and sewed over again. It was
hard work to sit down again, but the weary child
said to herself—

"I will try to be worthy of my name, as the lady
told me."

And so she began the hem afresh, finished it
neatly, and had an ungracious permission to go to
bed.

How she would have valued a kind, motherly kiss
that night, such as Martha Gibson's. None was
ever given her now.

But little Christian did not feel entirely lonely.
As she undressed herself, and folded up her things
neatly in the way her aunt liked, she knew that One
above cared for her; and she remembered what Mrs.
Clair had said about that great One having given her
her present life to bear, because in some way it would
be best for her. There was something so pleasant in
knowing that such an insignificant, lonely child as

herself was really being thought of and watched over. She had learnt at church that it was so, and the lady had reminded her of it.

Sleepy as she was, she would not for anything have missed saying her usual prayers; and then she fell fast asleep as soon as she laid her head down.

But her day's trials were not quite over yet. She had been in bed about an hour and a half, when she felt a rough hand on her shoulder, and her aunt's voice desired her to get up that instant.

It was some moments before she could arouse herself, so as to understand what she was to do. At length she found that she had forgotten to put away some work in a drawer which her aunt had given into her charge when she came to bed. She had laid it down on a table, and Miss Bonar's anger was aroused when she came up, and saw that her order had been neglected. She thought it would teach her to be more careful in future, so she aroused her out of her sound sleep, and desired her to rise and take the work to its proper place.

It was a great trial to temper, and Christian had hard work to be worthy of her name now. However, she kept back the tears and the grumbling words that rose to her lips, and quietly did what she was told. Miss Bonar was secretly sorry that she had been thus harsh about so trifling a neglect. She was beginning to feel the power of the meek obedience which, in her own little way, Christian was trying to practise.

CHAPTER III.

"Though closely upon us our troubles may press,
Let us try to help others in equal distress;
To do all in our power their griefs to abate,
Will help to relieve our own burden's weight."

EAGERLY did Christian watch the progress of the work Mrs. Clair had sent to be done, longing for the day when it would have to go back to her. The peep into that boudoir, and the conversation with the gentle lady, had seemed to her almost like a vision of fairy land. Mrs. Clair had said she should like to see her again sometimes, so she hoped that she should be sent for upstairs as before. What, then, was her disappointment when she heard Miss Bonar desire Patty, the kitchen maiden, to take the parcel, and return as quickly as possible.

Her aunt and she had so little sympathy together, that Christian had not said anything about her interview with Mrs. Clair, except as regarded the work.

2

But now she told her how much she desired to go
instead of Patty, and was so eloquent about the lady's
kindness, that she defeated her own purpose by making
Miss Bonar fear she might be forward and troublesome
if she went; so she was more than ever firm in her
resolve that Patty should be the messenger. Christian
fairly burst into tears as the front door closed behind
the girl, and she aroused her aunt's displeasure by the
careless, indifferent manner in which she sat down to
her appointed task, and at first took pleasure, rather
than otherwise, in provoking her.

But better feelings came soon, and she asked herself if this was being "worthy of her name"? And
then her fingers moved more rapidly, and her answers
to her aunt were submissive and humble when she
spoke to her.

But her heart was sad, for she knew it might be
weeks before there would be any message or parcel
again for Mrs. Clair. When Patty came back she
brought a note for Miss Bonar, who uttered an exclamation of surprise as she read it, and then looked
hard at Christian for a moment, as if hesitating whether to tell her its contents or not. Perhaps, too, she
was examining her to see what there could be in her

appearance which could so have attracted Mrs. Clair as to have produced the request contained in the note. It was to the effect that she should be very glad if Miss Bonar would permit her niece to go the next day to spend an hour or two at Mrs. Clair's house. If she could get there about four o'clock, Mrs. Clair would take care and send her away before dusk.

That lady was Miss Bonar's chief customer, and one whom she would, on no account, have offended, so she at once decided Christian should go, though she expressed her amazement pretty plainly at such a lady noticing a child like her.

Miss Bonar knew nothing of that spirit of love which actuated Mrs. Clair to seek out a little lonely girl, in the hopes of helping to brighten a life which appeared to be so trying for one at her age.

The next day Christian set forth, after receiving numerous parting admonitions from her aunt, as to what she was to say and do when spoken to. She found Mrs. Clair on the sofa as before, who received her with a smile of welcome.

"Come, Christian," she said, "I thought you and I should like to see each other again. Take off your hat and cape, and come and sit by me."

The little straw hat and white muslin cape were taken off and laid on a footstool in the corner of the room, because Christian thought it the humblest place she could find for them, and then Mrs. Clair made her sit down on a low seat by her side.

"Well," said she, "and how are you getting on ? Are you feeling any happier than when you were here before ?"

"I have tried sometimes to remember about being a Christian," replied the child, "but I cannot always."

"We none of us always do as we should, but if we watch and pray we shall be helped."

"It is very hard to be good when people are cross," said Christian, and a tear trembled in her eye.

"It is much easier, certainly, when every one is kind, and all things go smoothly," replied Mrs. Clair; "but there are very few persons who have not troubles to bear, and the more we have, the more we must seek for help from above to meet them bravely. When I feel unhappy, I find it a good plan to try and think about others who are still more so, and how much worse things might be."

"Indeed, ma'am," said Christian, "I do not think anybody can be more unhappy than I am now. I do not like my aunt at all, she is so cross; I am quite sure she does not love me. Oh, if she had but let me go to Australia with the others!" And the child's tears fell fast.

"But yet you have many blessings, Christian, and you must not forget them. Your aunt gives you plenty to eat and drink, does she not?"

"Yes, plenty," replied Christian.

"And I can see that you have good clothes, suited to your station in life. Then you live in a comfortable house, I suppose, and have a snug bed to lie on every night."

All this Christian acknowledged, but the mention of her bed reminded her of her aunt's waking her up to put away the work, and she could not reply quite cordially.

Mrs. Clair did not wish to make her talk about her aunt; she desired rather to lead her mind into a different and happier state by drawing her out of herself.

"Now, suppose, Christian," she said, "that you had to beg your bread, as many children do, and that you had only rags to cover you instead of this neat print frock, and perhaps only a hedge or a hovel to

lie under at night; you would be much worse off than
you are now. Perhaps, as you go home this evening,
you will see some such children as I have described;
and if you think of the difference between you, you
will understand how far less hard your own lot is than
theirs. Remember, too, that if your aunt is cross
sometimes, she has been a good friend to you; and
though not really an aunt, she has paid for your keep
ever since you lost your mother. Do not brood over
the loss of your kind friends the Gibsons so much,
but strive to please Miss Bonar, and leave all the rest
to God. You will soon grow happier."

And now Mrs. Clair told Christian to ring the
bell, and when the maid came she asked her to take
the little girl down to the housekeeper's room, that
she might have some tea.

Christian thought she had never seen anything so
beautiful as the house, for the maid gave her a peep
into the dining-room, which was hung round with
portraits of ladies and gentlemen. But the one Christian liked best was that of Mrs. Clair herself, dressed
in white, looking strong and well, and as she was
before the sad accident which had obliged her to lie
always on the sofa.

The maid noticed how she lingered before this picture, and asked her why she did so.

"I think it is because I love Mrs. Clair so, that I like to look at her," replied Christian.

"Everybody loves her who knows her," said the maid; "and no wonder, for she is always doing good in some way or another. When she was up and about, she used to be herself looking after the poor, and trying to see how she could best serve them. Now that she can't stir, she sends others to them; but she often has young ones like you to her boudoir, and talks to them just as she's been doing to you. No wonder they love her," she repeated, as she led Christian on into the housekeeper's room, where tea was set out for two or three of the upper servants.

They were all kind to Christian. It was no unusual thing for their mistress to send them a young visitor. She had various *protégées* whom she befriended —some from one cause, some from another—as the maid had said. She was one who was never so happy as when she was benefiting others. She spent much of her time alone, for her husband was a naval officer, and often at sea for a year or two together. She had no children, and could therefore follow out the natural impulse of her heart, to.do such good as lay in her power to "Christ's little ones."

Christian's sorrowful face had particularly struck her the day she brought home her aunt's work, and her history had aroused the pity of her gentle nature. It seemed sad that at her age she should suddenly be torn from those who had been all in all to her, and doomed to live with one who, though a relation, had evidently no affection for her, and merely took her from a sense of duty. But this was no case of poverty to be relieved. Nor would it be possible or right to endeavour to remove the little girl from Miss Bonar, whose intention was to bring her up to help herself, and who, by so doing, was preparing her to earn her own living at a future day.

But Mrs. Clair knew well that the way really to benefit Christian was by endeavouring to teach her to think less of her own sorrows, and more of those of others. Many a young person had learnt from her the lesson, that it is "more blessed to give than to receive."

When Christian came upstairs again, Mrs. Clair gave her one or two little books to take home and read, telling her she might come and change them for others when she pleased.

"You will find an account in one of them," said she, "of a little girl who was always trying to help others in some way or another. A Christian child should do this, you know."

"But," said Christian, opening her blue eyes in surprise, "*I* could not do anything for any one! I have no money, and I scarcely ever see anybody but my aunt, and Patty the servant girl."

Perhaps you will find ways in which you may be kind and useful to Patty. Look about you, and you will be surprised in how many little ways even one so young as yourself may be kind and helpful."

"Oh, I should be so glad!" exclaimed the child; "I should like very, *very* much to be of use to somebody;" and she unconsciously clasped her hands together in her earnestness.

"Then, suppose you begin and watch that you never let an opportunity escape you, however tiny a one it may be; and when I see you again you can tell me how far you have been successful. Now, good-bye, my child; it is time you went home."

Christian had made another friend, it seemed, in

that house, for the housekeeper called her into her room as she was going out, and gave her a present of a little parcel of sweet biscuits. Altogether, it was the brightest day she had had since the Gibsons went away from her.

CHAPTER IV.

"Self-denial, acts of love,
Words of mercy mild;
Goodness, gentleness, and peace,
Should mark the Christian child."

"BEGIN and watch that no opportunity escapes you."
These words of Mrs. Clair's Christian repeated to herself as she trudged home, and again and again she
thought—

"*I* can do nothing, *I* can show no one little kind-
nesses. I never see anybody but aunt and Patty."

As she was getting near her own home, a little
child passed her, meanly and scantily dressed, but she
did not excite her attention till she heard a cry,
and looking round, saw that she had fallen down,
and knocked her arm against an iron railing. There
was no one near except Christian and a young woman
carrying a parcel in her arms, who stopped and
good-naturedly spoke to the child, and examined

her arm. There was scarcely any mark to be seen, and the woman evidently thought she was crying a great deal more than the occasion required. "She cannot be hurt," she said impatiently, and she hastened on.

But the child continued to cry, and seemed hunting about for something.

"Are you hurt?" asked Christian, "that you cry so much."

"No," sobbed she, "but I have lost my penny," and fresh sobs followed as she continued to look on the ground.

Christian helped her to search, but it had evidently rolled away into some secret corner, and no efforts of theirs could find it.

"Was it your own penny?" asked Christian.

"No; mother gave it me to buy a penny roll for Tom's and my supper. We shan't have any now, for she hasn't got any more money."

"Are you hungry?" said Christian.

"Yes; I don't so much mind myself, but Tom is poorly."

There was no help for it. Christian could only say

how sorry she was, and then she walked away, thinking to herself—

" Now, if I had money of my own, like Mrs. Clair, I could give the little girl another penny, and even one or two more to make her happy. Oh, I wish I was rich !"

Suddenly she stopped. A thought had struck her. She *was* rich in one way, for had she not a packet of biscuits in her hand, and was it not in her power to give those to the child for herself and poor Tom ?

It was a great struggle. She had not even looked at them yet. The little girl was still seeking the penny, and not noticing her, so Christian sat down on a step, and untied the string of her little parcel.

Except in confectioners' windows no such tempting-looking things had ever met her eye as those which now lay in the paper before her. Biscuits of curious shapes and different sizes, some covered with beautiful pink and white sugar, others with comfits on the top. Christian liked cakes as well as any child ; these made her mouth water as she looked at them, and then they were her very own, given to her to eat herself.

" But you have had a good tea, and the little girl has had none," whispered something within her. " And

is not this your first opportunity of doing a kindness ?
Would it not be kind to give them to her ?"

It was quite a little fight went on for a few moments between Christian's liking for cakes, and her
wish to give them to the distressed child.

At last she made a compromise. She took out
several of the sugar-covered biscuits, tore off a piece
of the paper to wrap them in, and deposited them in
her frock pocket. Then going up to the little girl she
offered her the remainder.

They were received with delighted surprise, and
Christian noticed how thin and sharp her features were,
as if she were half-starved.

"You had better eat one directly," said she, and
she showed her a biscuit curled up like a snake, with
coloured comfits on it.

The child raised it to her mouth, but put it down
again amongst the rest, and shut up the paper.

"I'd rather not eat one here. I'd like to take
them to Tom."

"Where do you live ?"

"Close by, up Mercer's Alley."

"Is Tom your brother ?"

"Yes; but he's ill."

"Will he like the cakes, do you think ?"

"Oh, *won't* he !" exclaimed she.

"I should like to see Tom," said Christian, feeling a desire springing up in her mind to see how her present was appreciated by both the parties interested in them.

"Come, then," said she ; "it's scarcely a step," and she ran on before, looking back every now and then to see if her new friend were following.

It was to a wretched room in a small, close alley she conducted her. The house in which the Gibsons had lived, with its little shop in front, was as a palace compared to it.

There was scarcely any furniture, only a table, two chairs, and a few shelves. A stump wooden bedstead in one corner, and in another a small bed was made on the floor, and on this lay Tom.

"Oh, Nelly, Nelly, what a time you've been !" he exclaimed as soon as she entered ; "I thought you were never coming."

Nelly flew to his bedside.

"I lost the penny, Tom. I fell down and it rolled away, and I could not find it again. But look here," and she laid the biscuits on the bed before him.

The look of bitter disappointment that had gathered
on the poor lad's countenance at the first part of her
speech changed suddenly to one of pleasure and
admiration at the tempting sight the paper dis-
played.

"*She* gave them me," said Nelly, "and she's
come to see you, Tom."

Tom looked with a half shy, half grateful look at
Christian, who stepped forward and said, "I hope you
will like them ; please eat them up."

There was no need to repeat the request. Tom
seized one with the eagerness of a half-starved boy ; it
was gone in an instant, and Nelly pushed another into
his hand.

"That's yours," said Tom. "You've had none,
have you ?"

"No," said Nelly, "but I only want one, I'm not
so hungry as you."

There were six biscuits in the paper. Tom stoutly
refused to eat more than half, so stoutly that Nelly
yielded.

Christian's hand went into her pocket and drew
forth the remainder. She placed them, coloured sugar
and all, upon the bed, exclaiming, "There are some

'She gave them me,' said Nelly, 'and she's
come to see you, Tom.' *Page* 32.

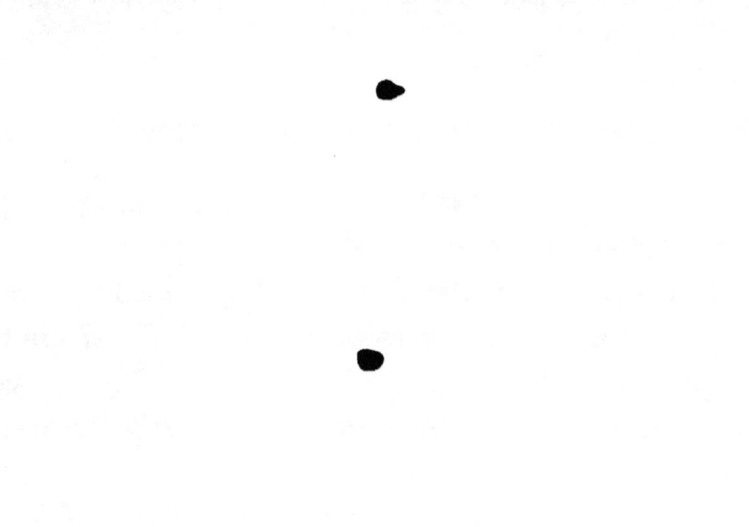

more; I like you to have them all," then turning away, she ran off as fast as she could.

It was a new and strange feeling that had come over her. She felt inexpressibly happy. Not a shade of disappointment at losing the biscuits alloyed her pleasure at having given them to those hungry children. And this pleasure lasted so long! The cakes would have been eaten up directly, but the thought of Nelly's delighted look, and Tom's grateful shy one, kept coming back all the evening afterwards.

Miss Bonar asked her a great many questions about what she had done and seen at Mrs. Clair's. Christian had to describe exactly what sort of dress the housekeeper wore, what pattern were the cups and saucers, etc., etc., till at last her aunt's curiosity was exhausted. "And where are the biscuits the housekeeper gave you?" she asked; "you have not eaten them all on your way home, have you?"

Christian explained how she had given them to the little brother and sister.

Miss Bonar looked at Christian with amazement.

"Why, you don't mean to tell me that you gave them away to the first brat you met?"

"But she looked so hungry, aunt; and she and her

3

brother would have had no supper, as she had lost the penny."

"Well, to my thinking, charity begins at home, and it is not every day you can have such things given you. I should have thought you wouldn't have been in such a hurry to get rid of them."

Christian did not know how to explain that she would have liked to eat them very much, and that it was not that she did not care for them she gave them away, but because she wished to begin and be kind to other people. She felt that her aunt would not understand her exactly, so she said no more about it, and the subject dropped. Those who have known what it is to have the pleasure of *giving*, will be able to understand that she went to bed with a happy heart that night. True, her offering had been but small, but it was all she had. She kept back nothing for herself, and He who accepted the widow's mite would not despise little Christian's first tiny deed of charity.

CHAPTER V.

"———— We must not care
About ourselves alone,
But freely give, or gladly share,
What might be all our own."

PATTY GRENFIELD, Miss Bonar's servant, had a hard life of it; not so much from being overworked, as, because it was so difficult to please a person of her mistress' irritable temper. She had an old grandmother, of whom she was fond, and who was her only relation, but she was in the most destitute circumstances, and had been glad to get her grandchild as servant of all work to Miss Bonar, with scarcely any wages; for, as she said, "the lass would at least get something to eat and drink every day." Patty was as ignorant a girl of fourteen as could be found anywhere; somewhat clumsy with her fingers, and not over bright; but she was good-tempered and willing, and anxious not to be a burden on her grandmother, who had an allowance from the parish, scarcely sufficient to support herself. Miss Bonar certainly often had provocation with her slow, awkward ways, and Patty, who was very humble-minded, was aware of this, and looked upon herself as fortunate to have been hired by her.

It was no part of Miss Bonar's plans to give Christian any of the housework to do. She did not wish her hands spoilt for dressmaking. "Patty was not worth her keep," she would say, "unless she could do enough to earn it." So she was rather jealous of Christian ever offering her any help.

The two girls had not, therefore, been thrown much together, as Christian was kept close to her needle, but Mrs. Clair's remark that perhaps she might be of some use to Patty, made her begin and think on the subject.

"I'll lend her the pretty story-book Mrs. Clair gave me," thought she; "that will be kind."

She put a paper cover on it, being terribly afraid of Patty's not over cleanly fingers, then took it to her in the evening, when she had not much to do.

"It's such a pretty story, Patty," she said, after telling how it had been given to her, "and I will lend it to you to read."

Patty was mending a pair of her own coarse worsted stockings with a huge needle. She dropped her work into her lap, opened her black eyes wide with surprise, and replied, "La, bless you, I can't read, not I."

Christian was very sorry to find that this first attempt of hers for poor Patty's benefit was a failure.

"Then you never went to school?" she said.

"No," said Patty. "Granny never had no money to spend on learning me, she says."

"I dare say you'd like to be able to read," said Christian.

"Yes, I'd like it well enough."

"I could teach you, if aunt would let me."

"Bless you, where's the time to come from? I'm always busy, except a bit of an evening."

"If I might help you a little with your work, you would get forward, and then we could have time enough," said Christian. "I wonder if my aunt would let me."

Patty shook her head doubtfully. She said it would be no use to ask. Things must be as they were.

" No harm in trying," thought Christian, and she watched her opportunity.

It came the next day, when she had just finished sewing some trimming on a dress so neatly, that Miss Bonar was pleased, and told her she might amuse herself for an hour in any way she liked.

" Then may I help Patty a bit ?" said she.

" Patty hasn't more than she can do; there's no washing to-day."

" I want to teach her to read, aunt; and if I might help her forward with her work a little every day, she'd always have time of an evening."

" But where on earth is the use of teaching her to read ? Her business is to scrub and clean. What good will reading do her ?"

" I think it will, perhaps, some day," said Christian, rather puzzled what to say in defence of her plan, yet convinced she had right on her side. " May I teach her, please ?"

" Do as you like, so that you neither of you neglect your work. You'll soon be tired of the job, I can tell you."

Probably she would have been, had the motive which made her attempt it been a less high one, for

Patty's powers of learning were small in the extreme. It seemed almost impossible to teach her the forms of the letters. Again and again Christian felt tempted to give it up. But she persevered, and at last symptoms of improvement encouraged her. Patty mastered the letters, and having done so, took more interest in the lessons than at first, when they appeared to her but as meaningless strokes, and after this the progress was tolerably rapid.

Patty's ignorance on all subjects, except her every day business as a servant of all work, was great. Beyond the fact that there was a God, and heaven, and hell, she knew little of religion. Christian found this out, and often wished she could go to the Sunday school.

She herself had formerly attended it with the young Gibsons, and she continued to do so now, as Sunday was entirely a leisure day with her. She had always liked it, but now it was her greatest pleasure, the one great break in the monotony of her life. She was very fond of her teacher, Miss Anson, and took real delight in preparing her Sunday lessons. Still more did she enjoy the pleasant hour before church, in the afternoon, when Miss Anson gathered her class round her, and read aloud some interesting book. It made Sunday the one bright day of the week to her. The thought of the change, and the rest it brought, helped her through many a weary hour's stitching in the little close workroom.

"If Patty could but go too," she often said to herself. "If she could but be taught by Miss Anson, as she had been for so long." But she could as little be spared on Sunday as any other day. Her aunt always lay in bed late on Sunday, and in the afternoon she generally went out to visit her friends, whilst Christian went to school and church, and Patty kept house. Then the latter went out in the evening for an hour or two, either to church or to see her granny, as she liked.

For her to go to the Sunday school was impossible, so decided Christian, as she lay awake one night after giving Patty a reading lesson, in the course of which the girl's ignorance on some simple religious point had been called forth.

"She could not be spared, of course; there would be no one to get ready her aunt's breakfast, or prepare the dinner, or wash up the dinner things, and keep house in the afternoon. No, it was out of the question, *unless*——"

Whenever Christian arrived at that portion of her thoughts commencing with the word "*unless*," she felt uncomfortable, and, burying her head deeper down in her pillow, tried to go to sleep. But somehow her eyes always opened again, and she went over the same train of reflections, the conclusion of which being very disagreeable, she tried to shut it out.

"*Unless*" she could get her aunt to let *her* do Patty's Sunday work, and so enable her to go to school in her place. A simple, feasible plan, but involving, oh! how much of self-denial and loss of positive happiness to poor Christian none but herself could know.

There was no other way of helping Patty in respect to her sad ignorance. But if her aunt would consent to such an arrangement, this plan, if carried out, might be the greatest help to her. And Christian felt that she ought not to shrink from effecting it if possible?

A greater fight went on within her than when

only the loss of a few biscuits was involved. So long and severe was it, that she thought she should never come to a decision as to what to do. She was generally asleep long before her aunt came to bed, but now she heard her beginning to move about, and knew she was putting away for the night, and that it must be late. Yet there she was, as wide awake as ever.

"I know what I'll do," she said to herself, "perhaps it will help me." And she slipped out of bed, kneeled down, and, hiding her face in her hands, she asked God to make her do what was right about poor Patty, and not think of what she liked best for herself.

Miss Bonar came up to bed about a quarter of an hour after, and found Christian fast asleep as usual.

The next day, to her great satisfaction, she was desired to go on a message to Mrs. Clair's. The lady was not at all well, and the doctor had advised her to keep perfectly quiet, but when she heard that Christian was below, she sent for her for a few minutes, knowing well how she prized these interviews, and being anxious to help and strengthen her in her efforts to act as a Christian child. It pained Christian to see how ill Mrs. Clair appeared; she lay looking to-day pale as a white lily, and almost as lovely. But she held out her hand to the little girl in her own sweet way, and asked her what she had been doing. And Christian told her all about Patty and the reading lessons, and then she confided to her the thought that had occurred about her going to the Sunday school instead of herself. A smile of inexpressible pleasure lighted up Mrs. Clair's pale features. She saw that the little girl was beginning to taste a happiness she had long known herself, and which would make her, in a great measure, independent of external circumstances.

"Do you think your aunt would consent to your plan?" she asked.

"I think perhaps she would, ma'am, for it would not really make any difference to her. I can do everything Patty does on Sunday."

"How many years have you attended the Sunday school?"

"Ever since I was quite a little thing, learning my letters," replied Christian. "I am nearly twelve now."

"Suppose it were to be managed for Patty to go in the morning, and you in the afternoon ?"

For a moment Christian's countenance beamed with pleasure at the thought of thus compromising the matter, and sharing with, instead of quite relinquishing to, Patty her precious Sunday pleasure. But a little thought on the proposal convinced her it would be far more to Patty's advantage to go both morning and afternoon to school, and she explained why.

"In the morning we say our collects and some texts," she said, "and in the afternoon Miss Anson reads us some story on the same subject as the texts or collect, so that the afternoon is only going on with the morning's lesson, though it is the pleasantest part of the two. I should not like Patty to miss it, for the stories make me understand the texts better than anything."

"But you must not give up going to church, Christian."

"Oh, no, ma'am. Patty can come home after school, if we explain why to Miss Anson, and she and I can take it by turns to go morning and afternoon, and sometimes I can go of an evening."

"Then I think you will be doing a right and kind thing, Christian, in giving up your privilege to poor, ignorant, untaught Patty. He who has put it into your heart will not let you suffer by the privation, I feel sure. When Christ was on earth, He was ever seeking the welfare of others, and we are told to make Him our example. In your own humble way you are trying to follow Him, and may God bless you, my child, and help you to do so more and more. She raised her head, and kissed Christian's brow as she sat beside her, and the child thought she was like an angel on earth; and, as with hushed steps she left the partially darkened room, a vague kind of fear arose in her heart, that she might soon be one of earth's angels no longer; and it comforted her to ask God to let Mrs. Clair live, if it should please Him.

When she reached home she told Patty of the proposed plan about the Sunday school. Patty liked the idea very much, but felt quite sure that Miss Bonar would not consent to her going. "She knew her too well," she said.

But Christian had hopes, because the proposed arrangement would in no way interfere with her aunt's comfort. She knew, too, that Mrs. Clair's name had great weight with her, and she could say how highly she approved of the scheme.

At first Miss Bonar treated it with ridicule. She said that she was making a fool of herself about Patty; and who ever heard of a servant girl going to a Sunday school. The girl was stupid enough as she was, without filling up her head with collects, and texts, and stories. But Christian stood her ground firmly, though gently. She pleaded that it would make no difference in the house whether she or Patty were at home, promised to do her part in the household matters diligently, and begged so eloquently, that at last Miss Bonar, who saw it was a matter of no importance to her, gave her consent, ungraciously enough, but Christian was too used to her manner to care for it. Patty was delighted, though rather shy at the thought of going.

Christian's next business was to go and see Miss Anson, and ask her to allow Patty to take her place in the class. And here arose a difficulty she had not foreseen. Patty, not being yet able to read, could scarcely be admitted to so high a class; but on Christian undertaking to read over the collect and texts to her, which would form the Sunday's lesson, Miss Anson said that she would excuse her from learning them. Sorry as she was to lose Christian, she could not but approve of what she was doing. No one knew better than she did how real an act of self-denial it must be.

So the following Sunday Patty went to school, and Christian took her place at home. She was rewarded for her first day's loss by the girl's expressions of gratitude and pleasure when she returned home.

CHAPTER VI.

"Where there's a will there's a way."

CHRISTIAN had not forgotten poor Tom and his sister Nelly, and one day, when her aunt sent her out for a walk, she thought she should like to take another peep at them, so she made her way to Mercer's Alley. In the same corner, looking paler and thinner than before, still lay the sick boy. He remembered Christian's face directly when she went in, after timidly knocking at the door; and the bright smile of welcome she received, set her at ease at once. No one else was there just then. Nelly was out, and the mother had got a little work to do by the day at some shop not far off.

"Are you no better, Tom?" asked Christian. "Are you still obliged to lie here?"

"Yes, I'm too weak to walk."

"It must be very dull work?"

"Yes, that it is; but Nelly sits with me."

"Does she read to you?"

"No, she can't; she's never learnt."

"Would you like me to read to you?"

"Yes, but I've no book."

"I'll come again soon, and bring a book."

"Will it be a story?"

"Yes; I've got several story-books, and one is all about a sick boy, who had to lie in bed, just like you."

"And what became of him at last? Did he get well, or what?"

Christian felt uncomfortable, for *her* sick boy had died, and she did not like to say so, lest it should frighten Tom. After a moment's pause, she said, "He did not get well; but he was very happy."

"Then did he die?"

"Well, yes, he did die," said Christian, getting quite red at the bungle she had made of it.

"I think I shall die too," said Tom. "I'm sure the doctor thinks so. It's the decline ails me, and people don't ever get well of that. Did your boy in the book die of decline?"

"I don't know, I forget; I think he did though,"

said Christian, feeling herself getting more and more into a scrape. She was afraid Tom's mother would be very angry if she found she had said anything to alarm him.

"Please bring the book," said Tom.

Christian promised, and just then Nelly came in, bringing with her a large ripe pear for Tom, which she said the fruit woman at the shop had sent him. The poor lad's hot, feverish lips showed how welcome it would be. How Christian longed to bring him some more! All the time as she walked home she kept thinking how she could get him some fruit. But she had no money, not even a penny. She told Patty that evening all about Tom, for the two girls often had a talk together after the reading lesson was over.

"If I could but earn some money," said Christian; "but there's nothing I can do."

"You can net," said Patty. "You might make some nightcaps and sell them, like that old woman that came here yesterday."

The idea was worth consideration, for Christian could net, knit, and crochet pretty well, but she had no cotton, and no pins or needles for the purpose. They were cheap enough. Sixpence would quite set her up as far as they were concerned, but she had not got it, and she would not dare to ask Miss Bonar for one. A day or two afterwards, Patty, who had been out on some errand, put her head into the workroom and made various grimaces at Christian behind her aunt's back, from which the former understood that she was to come into the kitchen for some mysterious reason. As soon as Christian appeared, she drew a small parcel out of her pocket, which, with a very clumsy, excited sort of jerk, she stuffed into her hand.

"I've got 'em," she exclaimed. "Now you can make the nightcaps."

The parcel contained a crochet needle and some cotton.

"Where did you get these from?" asked the astonished Christian.

"Bought them, to be sure."

"But where did you get the money?"

"Honestly enough. My bit of wages came in yesterday, you know."

"But, Patty, have you been spending them on me? And you were saving so for a new pair of boots!"

"Never you mind, I shall do very well. I've

got nearly enough to buy them, and I can wait a bit longer."

"I'll tell you what I'll do, Patty; I'll make a nightcap and sell it, and pay you back; there will still be plenty of cotton left for another."

"Indeed you *shan't* pay me back," said Patty, indignantly; "you must buy pears for Tom with the money when you get it;" and in her wrath at the notion of being "paid back," she let a basin slip from her fingers, which Christian fortunately caught before it reached the floor.

So the cap was begun, and progressed, although it was only at odd moments she could produce it from her pocket; how to dispose of it when finished was an important future consideration, and one which puzzled both Christian and Patty. The former began to feel her life a very different one to what it had been formerly, when the hours dragged listlessly by without interest in anything or anybody. Mrs. Clair had indeed taught her a valuable lesson, when she told her to benefit herself by trying to benefit others.

Miss Bonar was less cross to her now than she used to be. She found her uniformly industrious with her needle, and improving so fast, that she foresaw she would become a valuable assistant in time, and almost unconsciously she was beginning to feel an affection for the child who was thrown on her care, and who so studiously endeavoured to please her.

Christian did not neglect her promise to go and read to Tom. Her aunt generally allowed her to have an hour or two for her own amusement in the course of the day when she was not particularly busy, and so one afternoon she went with her story-book, and took her seat by his bedside.

Tom listened with great interest. He was getting weaker daily, and seemed to know that he should never run about and play again. He was not unhappy, but he wanted to talk to some one about that other world to which he felt he was going. His father was dead, his mother was obliged to be out all day in order to earn the few necessaries they had, so Tom was left to his little sister's care, and a neighbour looked in now and then. Hour after hour the poor boy lay on his little mattress on the floor, with no occupation, often feeling faint and weak from illness, or from want of proper nourishment. The doctor came sometimes, but he could do him no good. The child was wasting away slowly but surely.

His mother was kind, but she was an ignorant woman; ignorant, above all subjects, on that of religion. She had never asked any clergyman to come to see her boy. Tom had no one to talk to on that which was uppermost in his mind, "What sort of place would another world be?" But now he found Christian's story was of a child who had been like himself, and who had died as he was going to die. So he naturally listened with interest.

And then came questions to Christian, some of which she knew not how to answer, and some that she could reply to full well, thanks to Miss Anson's instructions in the Sunday school. But the burden of Tom's anxiety was to know how he could be quite sure that he, too, should go to heaven, as the boy in the story-book seemed to be satisfied that he should.

Christian was able to explain that Christ had died for all, and that trust in Him, and Him only, was the one sure hope; but she wished he could have better teaching than hers, so she resolved to tell Miss Anson about him. She went that very day, and the result was, that directly Miss Anson told the clergyman he was ill, he went to see him; and he led the boy on gently, step by step, till he no longer had any doubts or fears about the future, but felt happy in the conviction of a Saviour's love and care for all who sought Him, and placed their hopes of forgiveness on Him alone.

If Christian was kind to Tom, he was the means of benefiting her in return, in a way that was indeed precious; for, day after day, when she went to see him, they spoke together on these subjects, and Tom, whose shyness was all gone, loved to tell her and Nelly all about what Mr. Anson, the clergyman, said. He liked to have the Testament read to him better than a story-book, for it told him of Christ and his love, and that was all in all now to the dying boy.

Tom had more comforts than before, for Miss Anson took care that he should be looked after. Even Christian succeeded in persuading Miss Bonar to let her or Patty make a little pudding for him sometimes.

The hard crust of selfishness, which had grown over her heart, was softening gradually under the daily intercourse with this child, who was so often thinking of others. The incident of the biscuits had not been lost on her, although she had almost blamed Christian for her folly, as she called it. She had wondered and pondered, as she sat at her work, over her unselfishness

in sending Patty to school on Sunday, instead of going
herself, for she knew how she had always delighted
in it. The crochet nightcap, diligently worked at
whenever she had a spare minute, had not escaped her
attention; and when she found it was begun in hope
of earning a sixpence to buy fruit for a sick boy, she
began to think that Christian must be a very peculiar
girl, yet in her heart she felt a respect for her she
scarcely liked to acknowledge.

But she was mistaken in thinking Christian a peculiar child. It was simply the case that she had been led
by Mrs. Clair to open her eyes and look around for any
little opportunities of usefulness that might fall even in
her daily path; and where is the man, woman, or child
so circumstanced that none can be found? Few young
people could have had a more unvaried life than was
Christian's. She had no money, no influence, when
she went to live with Miss Bonar. Who would have
thought of looking for charity or deeds of kindness
from her? Yet she was beginning to be of importance to the happiness of Patty and poor Tom. She
had been the instrument of the greatest good to both,
by sending the former to school, and bringing a clergyman to the sick bed of the latter. And this was

effected simply by the desire having arisen in her heart to do something, however small, for the good of other people. May any children who read these pages stop for an instant, and think whether they cannot imitate Christian's example.

CHAPTER VII.

"God loveth a cheerful giver."

MRS. CLAIR's health did not improve. Whenever Christian went to see her (and she often sent for her), she fancied she looked a little paler and thinner than the time before. At last the doctors said she must go to a warmer climate for some time.

When Christian heard it, she felt almost as much as when told that the Gibsons were going to Australia. It seemed to her as if she no sooner began to love any one dearly than they were taken away from her. Even little Tom was likely to wing his flight for heaven.

"I shall not forget you, Christian," said Mrs. Clair. "You must write to me, and tell me how you are getting on; and all about Patty and Tom. I should like to leave you something to do for me, if your aunt has no objection; but it would take up a little time, and perhaps she could not spare you."

"She lets me have some time to myself almost every day," said Christian; "and she never refuses to let me do what you wish."

"There are a few old people who are bed-ridden in the workhouse, who love to be read to sometimes. I used to go myself to them when I was able, and since I have lain here, my maid has gone in my place. I must take her away with me, so the old folks will sadly miss their reading unless some one else can go. I have been thinking a great deal about it; and if you would like to go, and your aunt would not object to your doing so, I should like you to undertake it very much. You can read nicely, and I am sure you would like to feel you were of use to me and to the old people."

"Indeed I should very much," said Christian, feeling as though half the pang of separation would be gone, if she could be employed for Mrs. Clair.

"My maid goes twice a week generally," said Mrs. Clair; "perhaps you will not be able to go as often always, but I will myself see your aunt, and ask her about it."

Miss Bonar had to wait on Mrs. Clair soon after this conversation, about some new dresses, and she then talked to her of her little plan for Christian. It was in fact more on the young girl's account than on the old people's, that she proposed she should read to them, for she could easily have found an older person to undertake the office. But she wanted to carry on the good work that was being effected in Christian's mind, by continuing to draw out her sympathies for others.

, Miss Bonar did not object to the proposal, but her consent was not given so cordially but that it was evident there was a little dissatisfaction.

"You see, ma'am," said she at last, in reply to Mrs. Clair's request that she would tell her plainly what she felt, "Christian has been a burden to me ever since she was born. They were going to have taken her to the union, but I didn't like to have a relation of mine there, so I paid for her to be brought up, and now that she's getting a great girl, and is uncommon handy with her needle, I expect her to pay me back as it were."

"It is quite right and reasonable that she should do so. I hope and believe you will find her the greatest help to you as she grows older. But should you not be glad that she should be of some use to others also, if it does not interfere with the duties you require of her ?"

"I've no objection, I'm sure," replied Miss Bonar; "only it can't be expected that I'm to be a sufferer that others may gain."

For an instant Mrs. Clair felt almost disposed to tell Miss Bonar that she should say no more on the subject, but find some one else to read to her poor women; but then she recollected that even here she might do some good by endeavouring to show Miss Bonar that she was mistaken if she thought she was exempt from responsibility to her poorer neighbours.

"No one wishes you to be a sufferer," she said; "and I do not think that the short time I proposed for Christian to spend at the workhouse, one hour twice a week, would be felt by you, especially as Christian tells me you allow her some time to herself, part of which she would willingly give up. But even supposing you spared her from her work for that short time, do you not think it would be a satisfaction to you to feel you were making a small sacrifice for these poor old creatures? I do not think any one can feel themselves quite free from the duty of charity."

Miss Bonar stared at Mrs. Clair in some amazement.

"I am not rich enough to be charitable," said she. "I have not money to give away."

"No, but perhaps you might spare a little of Christian's time. Believe me, you will be no poorer for any help you may bestow on the poor, whether it be time or money. You know that the Bible says, 'He that giveth to the poor, lendeth to the Lord.'"

"Well, ma'am," said Miss Bonar, a bright thought striking her as to her own good deeds, "no one can say that I haven't done my share, when I've taken that girl and brought her up all at my own expense. I hope that may be counted for something, at all events."

"If you did it from really charitable motives, assuredly it will be," said Mrs. Clair.

She recollected with pain that Miss Bonar had just before asserted, she took Christian under her charge, because she did not like a relation of hers to go to the union.

Miss Bonar did not wish to offend Mrs. Clair about this matter of Christian reading to the old women, so she thought it best to comply with her wishes.

"Christian shall go to the union, ma'am, for an hour twice a week."

But there was a slight tone of annoyance in her voice which grated on Mrs. Clair's ear, and which brought to her mind the text, "Let no man give grudgingly or of necessity." She thought it better not to accept so unwilling a sacrifice, small as it was.

"You shall be no loser by her giving up the two hours a week," said she. "I will gladly pay eighteenpence a week to you in consideration of the work she would have done in the time she will be away. Will this be a satisfactory arrangement?"

"Thank you, ma'am, quite; I'm sure I would not take it, only one must live, you know; and time is money in a sense."

Mrs. Clair was too tired to say more, nor would it have done any good, she saw. She could only lift up a silent prayer, that He who could do all things, would give Miss Bonar the gift of a more compassionate and sympathizing heart.

As Miss Bonar walked home, she felt strangely dissatisfied with herself.

"What a fool I have been," thought she. "I might just as well have given up the girl for that short time without a fuss. And yet it's not unfair that I should have the eighteenpence a week. May be it's more than I'd get for the bit of work she'd do, but then she's a constant expense to me; so if she can bring me in a little in this way, 'tis but fair. Mrs. Clair would have paid somebody else if not her, no doubt. Yet somehow I wish I'd let her go for nothing; I'm half vexed with myself."

Her better nature was struggling against her love of gain. Which would have prevailed is perhaps doubtful, but affairs were about to take a turn she little expected.

CHAPTER VIII.

" We know not what a day may bring forth."

WHEN her aunt went out that afternoon to see Mrs. Clair, she gave Christian leave to go to Tom as soon as she had finished running some seams of a dress she was turning. She completed her task, put on her bonnet, and then took a silver sixpence from a little china cup on the mantelpiece.

It was her own sixpence, earned by the making of the nightcap. Patty had helped her to sell it, by taking it, when finished, to a woman who kept a poulterer's shop in a large way. Patty showed her the cap, and asked her whether she knew of anyone likely to buy it. "It's a good shape," said Mrs. Harley, taking it in her hand, " and an uncommon pretty pattern. I don't mind if I take it myself for my poor sick girl. It will please her to have it."

So saying, the good woman put her hand into her

5

ample pocket, and drew forth such a handful of silver and coppers, as seemed boundless wealth to Patty. She turned it over till she found a sixpence, which she gave to her, saying, "If that will buy it, I'll be the purchaser."

Patty closed joyfully with the bargain, and was just turning away, when a lady, who had come into the shop, and who had observed what had just passed, asked if she might look at the cap, the pattern of which struck her as light and pretty. She liked it so well, that she ordered one immediately; and Mrs. Harley, with whom she dealt regularly, said that if it was brought to her when finished, she would pay for it and forward it to the lady.

Patty rushed into the house in a great state of delight. Christian happened to be in the kitchen, and, not being aware that she had even taken the nightcap, she stared in amazement at her capers about the room, which greatly resembled those of a young bullock before a thunder-storm.

"What in the world has come to you, Patty?"

"Something that's a-going on to you," said she. Then opening her hand, she showed the sixpence.

" There, that's yours, not mine. I've sold your nightcap to Mrs. Harley, she's bought it for her sick girl ; and a lady who saw it has ordered another, so there's more money for you a-coming."

Christian's delight was equal to Patty's. A vision of ripe pears and oranges arose before her eyes for the poor parched, feverish boy. She longed to go off that instant to buy them; but it was getting late, and her aunt was calling to her to come to work, so she could only thank Patty again and again, and carefully deposit her little silver treasure in the china mug. It was on the following day that Miss Bonar gave her leave to go to Tom, whilst she was absent at Mrs. Clair's.

She took a little basket in her hand, and went first to a fruiterer's, where she selected three fine oranges, and then looked about for some pears.

But " they had none worth buying now," they said; and then her eye fell on some beautiful grapes —green and purple bunches, just arrived from the hothouse. She thought how even one of those would refresh poor Tom. Of what their price might be, she had no idea; but she just ventured timidly to ask if she could have any for threepence.

The boy who stood behind the counter grinned, and said, " He should rather think not." But the mistress of the shop spoke civilly to her, and said, " Grapes like those were too costly for any but rich people to buy; no others could afford to eat them."

" I did not want them for myself," said Christian, horrified at even a stranger thinking she had an eye on them for her own eating. " I was only thinking how a boy whom I know would like them. He is very ill."

" Poor fellow ! Here; I shan't be none the poorer for sending him one or two." And she broke off a little bunch of about eight grapes, and placed them in the basket. Christian's eyes sparkled with gratitude, and she offered to give her remaining threepence for them, which the woman indignantly rejected.

" Nay, nay ; I didn't mean you to pay for them," said she ; " take them, and welcome." Then gathering up one or two loose grapes that had fallen into the dish on which the large bunches stood, she added them to those already in the basket.

Christian could not thank her as she wished, for a livery servant came in at that moment to buy several large bunches of grapes for his master's table, and the woman's attention was engrossed directly.

Tom was more ill than usual to-day. His mother had not liked to leave him. She thought she saw a change for the worse. Little Nelly was, as usual, seated by his side, and her hand was clasped in his. The poor child was beginning to comprehend that her dear Tom was gradually slipping from her, and she liked to keep hold of his hand, as though she thought her doing so would prevent him from vanishing away.

Christian's appearance was always a welcome one to the children; and the poor anxious, toiling mother, herself far from strong, felt grateful to the kind-hearted, loving girl, who seemed to do Tom so much good.

Christian kneeled down by the bedside, and placed her little basket on the bed, so that Tom could see it.

" Look, Tom, what I've got for you. Three large oranges full of juice, and these grapes." And she put a large purple one to his hot lips, which opened eagerly to receive it. She continued to feed him with them, for she saw how they revived him, and she remembered there were still the oranges for another time. It was a pity that the kind-hearted woman who gave them was not by to see how refreshing was her little gift to the dying child. There were eleven grapes in all. He ate seven, and then asked them to save the other four for night, when he said his mouth got even more parched than in the day. Christian told how kind the woman had been in giving her the grapes, and Tom listened, and then said to his sister—

"Nelly, when we say our prayers to-night, let us remember to ask God to bless her."

Truly, as she herself had remarked, "she would be none the poorer for sending the few grapes to the sick boy."

Then Christian read a chapter in the New Testament, as Tom always liked her to do when she came. When she had finished, he told her that he had dreamed the night before that he was in heaven, and that everything looked so like sunshine there, that at first, when he woke, he felt quite disappointed; the more so because mother, and Nelly, and herself were all there too."

"I told Mr. Anson about it when he came," said he, "and how sorry I was it was only a dream. He said I must try to be patient, and I should soon be there. But I wish we were going together, instead of all of you coming afterwards."

"I don't think I shall be long after you," said the poor mother, whose hollow cough told that it was from her Tom inherited the fatal disease which was carrying him off. "I have feelings that tell me I shan't be much behind you. God grant I may go where you are going."

"Look to Christ, mother dear. He has saved me, Mr. Anson says, and He will save you, and then we shall both be with Him."

Nelly at this moment burst into a passionate flood of tears. They tried to soothe her, but at first in vain.

"Tom is going," she exclaimed, "and mother says she feels she is ill, and going too; and I feel quite well, and shall not be able to die, and I shall be left. Oh, mother! oh, Tom!"

Christian felt that she was the one who could best comfort her at present, so she dried her eyes and kissed her, and promised to try and be very kind to her, if ever the time came that she was left alone; and then, by way of diverting her thoughts, she set

her to squeeze the juice of an orange into a mug, that, with a little water and sugar added, Tom might have a nice cooling drink. In five minutes the child's tears were dried, whilst, every sorrow forgotten for the moment, she was engrossed in her novel occupation.

"I shall bring three more oranges in a short time," said Christian, "and some others after that; so do not spare these." And kissing Tom's forehead, and taking up her basket, the young sister of love left the room. She wanted to be home by their usual tea hour, and walked briskly on. Not far from home she saw a crowd of people which almost blocked up the street, so that she could not advance.

Some accident had happened, but what she could not tell, for she was not tall enough to see anything, and those around her seemed to know as little as herself. At last she heard that a woman had fallen down some area steps, and was a good deal hurt. She had been carried into the house, and a doctor was in attendance. He said she had better be taken to the infirmary, and a fly had been sent for. No one knew who she was.

A fly came up, momentarily dispersing the crowd

and Christian hoped she might now make her way, and pushed on; but the people closed up again, and she could not stir.

She was fretted by the delay, fearing her aunt would blame her for being late; but there was no help for it. At length she heard them say they were carrying the wounded person out, and placing her in the fly. Pity and curiosity made Christian strain her head to see her if she could, but there were too many tall people around. However, as the fly came near, and the crowd fell back to make way for it, she caught sight of a pale face which was leaning on the shoulder of another woman, whose arms were supporting her. The medical gentleman was sitting on the opposite seat, holding something to her lips. Her bonnet was off. It was but an instant's glance that Christian had before the fly passed out of her sight, but a dreadful idea struck her. That deadly pale face was very like her aunt's. She might be mistaken, for it was almost as white as a sheet, but the features were the same!

Her agitation was so great, that it attracted notice, and a woman asked her if she knew anything of the person who was hurt.

"I do not know; I am not sure," said Christian;

"but it seemed like my aunt. Oh, please, let me pass, that I may get home."

At this instant a man came running up the area steps on which the accident had occurred. He had a bonnet in his hand, which he said belonged to the poor woman, and he was going with it after the fly, which was moving at a slow pace down the street.

The woman who had spoken to Christian called to him that there was some one there who thought she would know to whom it belonged. The bonnet left no doubt on Christian's mind : it was Miss Bonar's.

The poor girl burst into tears.

"Nay, don't take on so," said her friend, who still kept by her side. "Maybe it's not so bad as you think. Come into my house for a moment, and I'll tell you all about it."

"But I must go after her directly," said Christian. "So you shall, but come in for a minute or two, till all these people have gone who stand staring at you now. She is in good hands, and you had better give them time to get her quietly into the infirmary before you or your friends get there."

The proposal was kind and good, and Christian

was not sorry to escape from the little crowd of children, and a few others who, having nothing to do, were watching her with curiosity, excited by her being somebody belonging to the person just taken to the infirmary.

The woman who asked her into her house was no other than Mrs. Harley, who kept the poulterer's shop, and who had bought the night-cap. The accident had occurred just in front of her house, on the opposite side of the street. She said that a light spring-cart had been coming down the street, containing groceries from a city shop. A Punch and Judy show was passing by, and the horse took fright, and began to be restive. The driver tried to hold him in, and succeeded in preventing his running away, but the animal backed suddenly on the pavement, where, unfortunately, Miss Bonar was walking. She gave a start to one side, and in so doing her foot slipped off the pavement, and went through an open area gate. She lost her balance, and fell from the top to the bottom of the flight of steps on to the stone flooring below. She was taken up insensible, carried into the kitchen, and a doctor sent for, who, as Christian knew, had taken her off to the infirmary, which was at some distance.

When Mrs. Harley found that Miss Bonar was a lone woman, with no one but Christian to be particularly interested in her, she was doubly kind.

"I don't see how a child like you can be going all alone to the infirmary," said she, "and it's getting late in the evening. We must be neighbourly, and do as we'd be done by in this world. I tell you what, if my man will mind the shop, and see to the late customers, I'll go with you myself."

Christian was very grateful, and asked to run home, just to tell Patty of what had happened.

"And you had better put up a change of linen for your aunt, my dear," said the motherly woman. "We can easily carry it with us."

Christian ran, for she could not walk, home. Quiet as she generally was, her nerves were now strung up to an intense state of excitement; and when she reached their house, she could scarcely tell Patty what had happened. Everything looked different to her somehow. There was her aunt's empty chair, with her thimble and pin-cushion on the table before it, and the piece of sewing she had been employed upon just before she left home, neatly folded, for she was always tidy, and could not endure confusion, as Patty knew to her cost, though greatly to her benefit.

All was the same as usual, and yet how changed. Would her aunt ever sit in that chair again ? Would that thimble ever be used more by her ? Might she not even now be *dead ?*

Patty tried to comfort her, but her own tears were falling fast, and she longed to go with her to the infirmary, and proposed locking up the house, but Christian reminded her how much her aunt would dislike it. Then they put up such things as they thought would be wanted, in a little bundle. Patty wanted her to have some tea, as the water was boiling, and all was ready, but Christian would not hear of it, and, taking leave of Patty, ran off with her bundle in her hand.

When she reached Mrs. Harley's, she found her looking out for her.

"Come in, child," she said; "you look as white and tired as possible, and you've a good long walk before you. You must have a cup of tea and something to eat first."

"Oh, no, thank you, please let us set off," exclaimed poor Christian, to whom every minute seemed an age.

"But tell me, when did you eat anything last?"

Christian was obliged to own not since dinner time, nearly six hours ago.

"Then not a step will I go with you till you've broken your fast. You are too excited and too young to be the best judge about what's best for you. It will not take long, and if you fall ill, which you are more likely to do than not, if you go a long walk without eating, who is to look after your aunt then?"

There was no denying the truth and good sense of her argument, so Christian followed her into a back room where everything was set out comfortably for tea.

But what caught her eye instantly, and at another time of less excitement would have aroused her warmest interest, was a sofa covered with a large patterned chintz which stood at one side of the room, and on which was seated a young girl about fifteen years of age. She was working, or trying to work, propped up with pillows.

"That's my Kate," said Mrs. Harley, and Kate

held out a thin hand to Christian, and said, in a pitying voice—

"I am so sorry for you, do take some tea."

"She's going to," said Mrs. Harley, in a tone of authority, for she saw that Christian was almost upset, and thought a little firmness the best thing for her.

Then she poured out some tea, and when she had drunk a little, she made her take a slice of bread and butter, and though it almost choked her, Christian made an effort and got through it.

"And now we will go," said Mrs. Harley; and charging Kate not to sit up till her return, if she were late, and her husband not to forget he was in charge of the shop, they started off.

"Kate has never been well since she had the scarlet fever a year ago," said Mrs. Harley, as they walked along. "She is so weak she has to lie in bed all the morning, and gets up and is on that sofa the rest of the day."

When they had reached the infirmary they found it was past the regular hour for the friends of the patients to be admitted, but on hearing that they belonged to the woman who had been lately brought in, they were shown into a waiting-room.

Miss Bonar was less seriously injured than had been feared at first. Her head had escaped, but her shoulder was dislocated, and she was severely bruised in other parts. As far as they could judge there was no internal injury.

This was the report brought to them; but to Christian's bitter disappointment she was not to be allowed to see her that night, as the doctors had been putting in the shoulder, and she was just laid quietly in bed, and must on no account be excited.

Christian shuddered at the thoughts of the pain she must have suffered when the shoulder was set, and to her relief and astonishment was told that she knew nothing about it, as she was under the influence of chloroform.

The nurse informed her that Miss Bonar had been told she was come, that she sent her her love, and should expect to see her to-morrow. She sent her her keys, and hoped she and Patty would be good girls.

This message comforted Christian, as it showed that her aunt was able to think of things as usual; and she left the infirmary in better spirits than she came.

Good Mrs. Harley saw her safe to her own door, and made her promise to go the next day, after she had been to the infirmary, to tell her how Miss Bonar was; and she offered any help or advice in her power to Christian and Patty whilst they were left alone.

CHAPTER IX.

" They also serve, who only stand and wait."

WHEN Christian arrived at the infirmary the next day, she was conducted up a wide flight of stone stairs, then along several passages from which she could see the long rows of beds in the different rooms, till she arrived at one where there was accommodation but for five occupants; and here, on a bed standing by itself in the farthest corner, lay Miss Bonar. Little outward demonstration of affection had hitherto passed between them, but things seem altered. Christian felt that her aunt had indeed acted as a relation to her, and that had she been killed by the fall, she would have been left alone in the world. Miss Bonar's heart drew strongly now to the child who was the only being who would have missed her. Many thoughts had passed through her mind as she lay awake during the night.

The conversation with Mrs. Clair was fresh in her

mind. She had spoken of her responsibilities to her poor neighbours; she *felt* now that she was right, conscience told her she was, and that she had been leading a sadly selfish life, thinking only of herself. She saw in its true light, her covetous acceptance of the money for Christian's time whilst she read to the poor women. She hated to look back on the past. She could not deceive herself now. Death had been too near: he had almost siezed her in his grasp. The pain she was suffering kept reminding her of this. She was glad when morning came: these thoughts were less vivid, less painful then, but they still haunted her. Christian's sweet placid young face was pleasant to look at after such a night as she had passed; never had their lips met in such affection before.

Only a very short time was allowed them, for the patient was inclined to be feverish.

"You will come and see me often, Christian," said her aunt; "it is dreary work lying here. I can't think how you and Patty will get on all by yourselves; oh dear, oh dear, when shall I get home again?"

"I will try and do all you would wish at home, dear aunt, and so will Patty. Try and not fret."

"How can I help it, to think of such an accident

happening to me, and keeping me here day after day, as I shall have to be kept, and all my work standing still, and no one to look after you girls;" tears prevented her saying more.

Christian kissed and soothed her by telling how kind Mrs. Harley had been, how she came with her the evening before, and had promised to help and advise them.

"I want to send a message to Mrs. Clair," she said; "tell her, Christian, that I see things differently to what I did when she spoke to me yesterday about your reading to the old women, and that I shall be *glad* for you to go, and I would rather she did not pay me for your time."

Christian promised, though she did not quite understand the latter part of the message. The nurse came up soon and said she must not stay any longer; so she bid her aunt good-bye, promised to tell Patty to keep her places tidy, and received a few other parting directions; and then she walked back through the long passages, looking with wonder and pity at the number of patients. She felt amazed at the vastness of the establishment, and the perfect order of everything she saw. She could not help wishing poor

Tom was lying on one of those comfortable beds, with everything supplied him that he could want, instead of upon his little hard mattress on the floor, with few comforts of any sort. "But Tom will soon be in heaven," she thought; "and then how little it will have signified about his having been so poor here."

She went according to promise to tell Mrs. Harley about her aunt. That good creature insisted on her taking some dinner with them, "Kate would be so charmed," she said, "for she scarcely ever spoke to a young person."

Kate was indeed glad to see her, and the girls soon got into conversation. Kate told her new friend about her illness, and how the weakness it had left obliged her to be quite an invalid. "But I like working," she added; "I can sew and knit, but I have never learned to crochet, and I want to, for I should like to be able to make a cap like this." And she produced Christian's own cap from her work-basket.

Christian recognized it directly; she remembered that Patty had sold it to Mrs. Harley.

"I can teach you to crochet," she said; "and I

know very well how this stitch is done, for I made this cap myself."

And then she explained how she had wanted money to buy fruit for poor Tom, and had tried the night-cap plan at Patty's suggestion, and how delighted they had been when Mrs. Harley bought it for Kate. This led to an account of Tom, and about Christian's first acquaintance with him. And then the conversation glided to her·acquaintance with Mrs. Clair, and how that lady had first aroused the desire in her heart to do Christian deeds worthy of her name. Kate listened with almost breathless interest. A longing was arising in her to be useful too.

"What a nice name you have," she said to Christian; "I wish I had been called Christian instead of Katherine: if I had, I should have wanted to do kind things too."

"But what difference would that make?" said Christian, opening her blue eyes so wide with surprise, that Kate laughed. "Your being named Katherine does not make it a bit less right for you to be kind."

"No, I suppose not; but I think being named Christian, as you are, would make one often think about it."

" But though you are not named Christian, you are a Christian, you know, because you were made one when you were christened. I remember Miss Anson telling us that one day."

"Well, I am sure I should like to be of some use; but I don't see how I can. You see, you were walking down the street when you met Nelly and helped her to look for her penny; but I have not been out for ever so long. I hope I shall get strong again, and able to go out soon."

"I hope you will," said Christian. Then, after a pause, she continued, " I remember something Mrs. Clair said to me one day, which I think you will like to hear. She was telling me about some poor woman she used to go and read to when she was strong and well, but who she had not seen for a long long time, and she said what a trouble it had been to her at first to be laid up on the sofa. She thought she should never be of any more use to anybody. But then she remembered that if God had work for her to do, He could as easily bring it to her as send her to it, only she must be on the watch for it, even more than before."

" And did God give her work?" asked Kate.

" Yes, a great deal," she said.

" Do you know what ?"

"I only know for certain about myself. She had me upstairs quite accidentally, to give me a message for my aunt about a dress she was making for her; and then she asked me all about myself, and when I told her my name was Christian, she asked me questions to find out if I knew what the word meant, and she talked to me, oh, so beautifully ! and she has been trying to make me a good girl ever since. Her maid told me she had other children into her room to talk to sometimes, so she has got work, you see."

" Ah, but it is so different for her; she is a lady, and grown up, and can do those sort of things; but it is quite different for me. Do you see any I can do, Christian ?"

Christian thought for a little while, and wished something would suggest itself; but at last she was obliged to shake her head and say she knew of nothing.

"You will come often and see me, will you not?" asked Kate, when Christian was tying on her hat before going away.

" Yes, indeed, I will, if I shall not be in the way."

" Not a bit," exclaimed Mrs. Harley, who had

entered the room as she said the words; "it will be a real kindness in you to come and sit with Kate a bit when you can: it's so lonesome for her, poor child."

Christian promised again, saying how much she should enjoy it, and then she left.

"I declare that's about the dearest little creature I ever saw," said Mrs. Harley, when she was out of hearing. "So quick and yet so quiet in her ways, and quite beyond her years in sense. I'll be bound she'll be as steady and managing as a woman whilst her aunt is in the infirmary."

"And she is so kind, mother; she's been telling me about a poor boy she goes to see very often, who cannot live long;" and then Kate told her mother about the nightcap, and how she made it in order to buy fruit for Tom. "She didn't tell me in the very least as if she was proud of it, mother; she seemed to think it was quite a favour to be able to do it, because she says a lady has taught her that every one ought to be doing something to be useful."

"Every one that *can*, I suppose, she means," said Mrs. Harley, and she smoothed the bright hair on her young daughter's forehead as she spoke; "but some

aro not able, you know;" and Kate knew she was
thinking of her.

"It's very hard, mother, to have to be always shut
up so; do you think I shall ever get quite well and
able to go about like Christian, so as to do as she
does?"

"I think you will, dear. The doctor says you are
getting better every week now, though one does not
see it; but it must be some little time yet before
you will be able to walk about like any one else."

"Then there is nothing I can be doing?" said she,
sorrowfully, and in a fretful tone.

"Kate, I'm no great hand at talking on these sort
of things; but I do think it is pretty plain that all you
can do is to be patient."

"But that's not doing anything, mother;" and the
tone of voice was more petulant.

"Yes it is, Kate; it's doing a good deal to bear a
hard trial bravely, and without complaining, because
Providence has seen fit to lay it on us. He can
remove it; but we must wait his time, you know."

Mrs. Harley was, as she had said, no great talker
on these subjects, but she thought more than she
spoke about them. She and her husband were

superior sort of people in their way. They drove a prosperous, thriving trade, and were laying by money. They had a married son, who had a good-sized farm in the country, from whence they got the excellent butter, poultry, eggs, bacon, etc., which had brought their shop into such great repute. It was, in fact, their own farm, but they preferred their son' living at it whilst they did business in London. Their prosperity had not hardened Mrs. Harley's heart. She was always ready and really glad to do a kind turn if she could, as she had shown in Christian's case the day before. She led a busy life, but she could open her heart to other things besides her shop and its concerns. Kate's illness was a great trial, and she felt it so, but sincerely desired to look upon it in a spirit of submission, and to teach Kate to do the same.

At tea-time Kate's eyes looked a little red. Her mother noticed it, though she said nothing; but she was half afraid her acquaintance with Christian might unsettle her, and make her feel her own situation more than before. She thought she had been crying because she could not walk out. But she understood better how things really were when, after tea, Mr.

Harley having gone out, Kate said, as she drew her mother down to kiss her, "I am sorry I was cross this afternoon, mother dear. I will try to be patient."

"Do, dear. It's tiresome work, I know; but you'll soon be able to go down into the country, and there you'll grow as strong as ever. I was afraid you'd been fretting because you couldn't go about like Christian."

"No, mother, it wasn't that; but I spoke crossly, and I was vexed with myself."

Kate felt happier now than she had done all the afternoon.

CHAPTER X.

"She was,
With gentle words and smiling face,
A sunbeam in that lowly place."

Mrs. Harley was quite right in supposing that Christian would be "steady and managing" in her aunt's absence. She was careful to act exactly as she would have done had she been there. But neither she nor Patty liked their new responsibilities, or the entire freedom to manage things as they liked. However much young people may fancy they should like to be rid of all restraint, yet whenever it so happens that circumstances oblige them, for a time, to rely entirely on themselves, they invariably end in soon desiring to have stronger minds than their own to lean upon. God has appointed that the young shall be dependent for advice and guidance on those who are older, and His laws are always wise and good.

Patty dreaded Miss Bonar's constant complaints

about her untidiness when she was at home; but now that she might throw her duster down where she liked, and hang up her dress on a peg in the kitchen instead of taking it upstairs, without a word being said to her, she found that, somehow, it was not pleasant to be left so much to her own habits, of which she herself thought less well than when Miss Bonar was there; and more than once scolded herself aloud when she had done some careless or slovenly thing.

Christian's time was pretty much taken up in one way or another. She found that she could finish some of the more simple jobs of work that were left undone. She had a dress to make for herself, which her aunt had cut out and tacked together for her the very day before her accident. Her daily walk to the infirmary took up a considerable time, and then there was Tom always so pleased to see her whenever she could go to him. She was anxious also to visit Mrs. Clair again, and to receive her instructions about reading to the old women. Time did not hang heavy on her hands; yet, like Patty, she felt it was pleasanter to be under the direction of another person, rather than quite her own mistress.

Miss Bonar progressed favourably but slowly. She was not in such haste to be removed to her own house as might have been expected, and was quite willing to stay as long as the medical men thought right. Perhaps she was aware how superior was her present nursing to what she could have at home, even with the best will on Christian's and Patty's part. She was not dependent on her dressmaking, as we before said; she had a little capital of her own, which made her tolerably independent, though it was not sufficient by itself. Her mind was not, therefore, in any pecuniary anxiety, from the sudden cessation of her work. She felt great dependence on Christian's good sense respecting the management of things at home. Her accident had weakened and shaken her so much, that it was rather soothing to her to lie in such perfect quiet as reigned over the infirmary. She read more than she had done during her whole life before, having plenty of books supplied her; but the one she perused most was the Bible. Christian generally read her a few verses when she came, and then she would go on from where she had left off, when she went away. As many have done before her, she found herself more engrossed and interested the more she

read. God was teaching her great and deep things
on her sick bed. His lessons were so absorbing her
mind, that she almost dreaded returning to her every-
day life. Now and then Patty begged leave to go
and see her. She was surprised to find how much
affection there was in the heart of this simple girl.
She had never shown her much kindness, considering
always that she did her full duty towards her by giving
her sufficient food, and such small wages as would
barely suffice to clothe her. But of any other responsibilities connected with her, as an orphan, almost
destitute of friends, who was thrown on her care, she
never thought. Christian, a mere child, had done far
more than she had, by sending her to school on
Sunday. Many a harsh and fault-finding word had
passed from her lips to poor clumsy Patty; seldom
an encouraging or cheering one. Yet the girl seemed
so full of sympathy and kind feeling towards her, that
she could not find words to express herself, except by
a burst of tears, when she first came to her bedside,
and the exclamation of " Oh, my poor dear missus,
my poor dear missus, I have been so sorry for you."
Miss Bonar was much touched. She had not expected
such genuine feeling as this, and for herself, too!

Henceforth Patty took a different place in her estimation.

The girl was eager to assure her mistress that everything was going on at home as she would wish.

"I've given the house a right thorough good cleaning, missus, from top to bottom, and I've not broken so much as a tea-cup; and I'm growing so tidy, you'd scarcely believe it's me. I dust and right-up all day long, I do. The fire-irons are polished so that they're quite a picture to look at. Oh! missus; but indeed the house is just beautiful clean."

"I quite believe it, Patty, for I know you have been trying hard to please me."

"I hope you'll soon be coming home, missus. Christian and I mean to nurse you a sight better than they will in a 'firmary."

Miss Bonar doubted it in her heart; but she did not say so. She spoke kindly to Patty, and bade her good-bye so affectionately, that the girl told Christian she never did see anything so kind as missus had grown since her accident.

There was a very respectable woman lay in a

7

bed near to Miss Bonar, whom she sometimes talked with a little.

When Patty had gone she remarked to Miss Bonar, " One can see that you've been a real good mistress to that girl. How fond she is of you ! Well, I do like to see people try to think of something for their servants besides getting all out of them they can."

Miss Bonar did not reply ; she felt each word almost as a dagger. She knew how little she deserved such praise.

Mrs. Clair sent for Christian a few days after Miss Bonar's accident, and told her that as she was to be allowed to go to the workhouse, she should like her to be accompanied by her maid the first time, that she might start her in her new office. Christian told her all that had happened, and delivered Miss Bonar's message about not wishing to receive payment for her time.

Mrs. Clair could not but hope that God was working a change in the heart of this woman, though He was doing so by affliction. If so, what a blessed thing would her accident have proved !

Christian had a great deal to tell Mrs. Clair to-day about her poor aunt, and she ventured to mention her new friend, Kate Harley, and her wish to be useful; but that she could not, confined to the house and sofa as she was.

"I told her," said Christian, "I had heard you say that God had brought work to you after you were ill. But Kate said it was so different with you, who are a lady, and can do so many things she is not able to."

"Take Kate a message from me," said Mrs. Clair. "Tell her that it is God's will that *some should work, and some should wait.* It is evidently His pleasure that she should *wait.* It may not be so pleasant as working, but if she is patient, and submits without a murmur, because it is His will, it will be equally pleasing to Him, and in good time He will give her something to do. Can you remember my message, Christian?"

"I am sure I can," she replied; and Mrs. Clair saw by the intelligent and feeling look, that she had caught the real meaning and spirit of her words.

Christian felt rather shy at first, when she arrived at the workhouse, and heard Mrs. Denton (as the maid was called) tell the matron that she was the young girl whom Mrs. Clair wished to come and read to the poor bedridden women. She wondered how she should ever find her way all through the passages by herself as she saw Mrs. Denton did. Then the women she met looked so odd in their workhouse dress. Altogether, she did not half like it, and, as she followed Mrs. Denton, she almost wished she had not come, and still more that she had not to do so again, and that too all by herself. But her fears, if such they could be called, vanished when she entered the long, clean room, with its rows of beds side by side, in two or three of which lay the old women, with their coarse, but clean, nightcaps, whilst several more sat in high-backed rush chairs round a comfortable fire.

The poor old bodies knew that Mrs. Denton was going abroad, and were bitterly lamenting over it day by day. The smallest events become great ones to those who have no change in their daily lives, and small pleasures and small trials (as they would appear to be to others) are, from the same cause, magnified into very great ones. Mrs. Denton's visits had so long been looked forward to with interest, that they really dreaded the loss of them, and some were almost disposed to think themselves hardly used that she did not stay behind for their sakes.

Old people are apt to become selfish, especially if

such has been the bearing of their characters when young; and this is one amongst other and higher reasons why thoughtfulness for others should be cultivated in early life, for a selfish old age is never a happy one.

There were two old people whom any stranger would have remarked, for the sweet serenity that rested on their aged faces: they were named Betty Banks and Molly Parsons. Betty had had a rheumatic fever long ago, which had left her without the use of her lower limbs, so she was always in bed. Molly had suffered from the same disease, though not as severely, yet sufficiently so to be bedridden. They had known each other long before they met in the workhouse. Quite a friendship had sprung up between them years ago, and the love of their old age was like that of youth. Both had seen better days; both had laid all their kindred in the dust, and were left to desolation and poverty, as far as this world was concerned; but both had sought and found that Saviour who was more to them than all they had lost.

Of Him they dearly loved to speak to each other, as they lay side by side, for their beds were drawn close together. They were both upwards of eighty years of

age, though still in full possession of their mental facul-
ties, and both were looking forward to living with Christ
ere long for ever.   At the first sight of these two dear
old women, Christian's heart bounded towards them.
She thought them very much alike, but this was because
each face was so thin and pale, and each had snow-
white hair peeping from under the large frills of their
caps, which were fastened on their heads by a band
of black ribbon, with a bow in front.   Their features,
however, were quite different, though both must have
been handsome when young.   The only real like-
ness lay in the gentle, contented expression, which
piety and repose had gradually spread over their
countenances.

It was to these two old women that Mrs. Clair had
first paid her weekly visits, and to whom she had sent
Mrs. Denton when no longer able to go herself; but, by
degrees, two or three of the fireside set, also aged folks,
began to like to draw near and hear the reading, till at
length they prized it as we have said—so highly, that it
was quite a sorrow to them to think that it must cease.

But when Mrs. Denton led Christian forward to
them, and said she was coming as often as she had
done, if possible, in order that they might still be read

to, their delight and gratitude almost overwhelmed Christian.

"God bless the darling!" were the words she heard on every side; and for some moments the poor old souls could do nothing but look at her through their spectacles, and speak aside to one another about her " sweet face."

If Christian heard their remarks, certain it is they did her no harm. She possessed in a high degree that beautiful gift in a child, *humility*. It was in a great measure natural to her character, and it was being strengthened and fostered by the blessed spirit of charity, that was taking such deep root in her young heart. Her only thought, on hearing the gratitude expressed by the old women for her proposed services, was, how very fortunate that she had been selected by Mrs. Clair for such a delightful task as making them so happy.

Mrs. Clair had noticed this trait in Christian's character. She saw that she was not a child who would be puffed up with ideas of her own importance, and therefore had not feared to fix upon her as her deputy in this matter. Her youth (as she could read nicely) she considered no drawback—rather an advantage, under the circumstances; for she knew how old age likes to be noticed and cared for by childhood, and she fully expected that Christian, with her engaging ways and humble manners, would soon win the hearts of the old folks, and would smooth and brighten the last steps of their rugged journey home.

She was right. Christian's workhouse mission did indeed grow to be one of love. Mrs. Clair gave her a large Bible, which was kept on a shelf at the foot of Molly's bed. She always placed it carefully there herself when she had finished reading, and some of the old women delighted in keeping it nicely dusted. Indeed, so much did they think of this little matter, that they were apt to quarrel sometimes as to which should have the charge of it.

From that first day's visit with Mrs. Denton it became almost the greatest pleasure of Christian's life to visit her aged charges. She soon learnt her way through the long passages, no one heeding the little, quiet, noiseless figure that was often seen gliding along to the women's sleeping-ward. But what a welcome always awaited her there! The old creatures would hobble a little way down the long room to meet her, the moment she appeared at the

'It became almost the greatest pleasure of Christian's life
to visit her aged charges.' *Page* 104

door, and came tripping towards them with her bright beaming smile. How pleasant was the greeting ever ready for her from Molly Parsons and Betty Banks, whose looks of love perfectly beamed out upon her as she stood first at the bedside of one and then of the other; for neither of them were satisfied unless they had taken her hand into theirs for an instant. Then Christian used to untie her little brown hat, hang it on a peg, and lift down the Bible, whilst one of the women always placed a three-legged deal stool at the foot of Molly and Betty's beds, just between the two, and the others came and sat as close as they could. As the Bible was rather large, Christian used to lean it against the foot of one of the beds, and then finding the place where she left off, she began to read in her young, clear voice. She could not go on fast, like a person more accustomed to read aloud; but this was all the better, and enabled the old folks to follow her easily, for she did not hesitate, unless it were at a very long word, and she minded her stops; so her slow reading was just what they liked. Now and then one of them would make a remark on a text, and another would say something in reply; and Christian always waited patiently till they had done, before she

went on again.   Sometimes, indeed, these little passing talks went on so long, that they would have taken
up too much time, as she had to leave at a certain
hour ; but then Betty or Molly used to say, very gently
and kindly—

"We had better let the darling read on."   And
they would stop directly, and Christian took up the
text at which she had left off.

There was a great clock at one end of the room,
and as soon as the hand reached the hour when she
knew she must go, she put a marker into the place,
laid the Bible on the shelf, tied on her hat, and
then bid her aged friends good-bye.   They thanked
her, and blessed her, and toddled back to their seats
round the fire.   Her last farewell was always given to
Molly and Betty.   She loved to hear them say, as they
always did—

"The Lord bless thee, and keep thee, dearie !"

Christian would not have missed those parting
words for anything.   They were not uttered like mere
words, of course, but as if the speakers really and truly
were at the instant praying to God for His care to be
over her, and that He would take her into His keeping; and so they were : for these two holy women

never uttered His name without a feeling and gesture of reverence, which was in consequence of their sense of its greatness.

Mrs. Clair was well satisfied with the success of her plan, of which she was enabled to judge before she left England, from the account brought her by Denton, who went to the workhouse just to bid farewell, and to take them a few comforts from her mistress. Christian had then been two or three times, and the account given of her visits convinced Mrs. Clair that she had provided a proper substitute in her maid's place.

One only anxiety she had, about which she wished to caution Christian. She was desirous that no *home* duty should be neglected by her, in consequence of her interest in her new employment. She had a conversation on the subject when the little girl came on the evening before her departure to say good-bye.

"Remember," said she, after listening with pleasure to her recital of her several visits to the workhouse, "that circumstances may arise to make it less your duty to go than to stay away sometimes. Should your aunt want you at home at any time when it is your day for the women, you must at once yield to her

wishes, and cheerfully give up.   Denton has explained
to them, that although you will go as regularly as
possible, yet things may often happen to prevent you;
and they quite understand this, and will be satisfied
that there is good cause for your absence."

"But my aunt has promised I shall go regularly,"
said Christian.

"And I feel sure she will keep to her promise: the
message you brought me from her the other day
showed me that she is anxious to do so; but it may
be impossible, or at least very inconvenient, at times
to spare you."

"But," pleaded Christian, whose heart was with
her old people, "would it be right in my aunt to stop
me from going merely to help finish a dress, or something of that sort?"   She was secretly afraid that
such contingencies might too often arise.

"The question in such a case would not be whether
your *aunt* was doing right, but whether *you* were,"
replied Mrs. Clair. "Your duty would be plain, it
would be that of obedience; and it should be cheerful,
willing obedience—no sullenness or ill-humour must
be shown, or more harm to yourself than good to the
old women might be the result of your employment.

Will you promise me to try and think of all this when I am away. I am the more anxious because your aunt's accident may make her very dependent on you for some time."

Christian promised, and then Mrs. Clair took out a sovereign, and putting it into a small purse, she gave it to Christian.

"I should like to leave this sovereign with you," she said, "that in case poor Tom needs any little comforts, you may be able to get them for him; and other objects of need and charity may come in your way, which I should wish you to be able to relieve. You had better consult your aunt and good Mrs. Harley as to the wisest and best methods of laying it out."

" Shall I buy anything for the old women sometimes ?" asked Christian, who feared they would miss the presents of tea and sugar which Mrs. Clair was in the habit of sending them.

" No ; I have desired my housekeeper to look after them, they will want for nothing that they have been accustomed to."

And now Mrs. Denton came in to remind her mistress that she had to travel on the morrow, and to beg her not to fatigue herself. So the parting moment was really come, which the little girl had so long dreaded.

"I shall often think of you, my child," said Mrs. Clair, "and I shall pray that you may grow up a good and useful woman."

"But you will come back before I am a woman," said poor Christian, startled by her words, and almost choked by her efforts to keep back her tears.

"If it please God that the warm climate I am going to does me good, I trust I shall return before very long in better health," replied Mrs. Clair. "All is in His hands; but I shall long to come back again, if it be His will to let me."

She put a little parcel into Christian's hands, and told her to keep the present within for her sake. Then, pressing her lips on her cheek, she bade her farewell.

Christian scarcely knew how she got so calmly from the room, down stairs, and out of the house. Her feelings were naturally very strong, and she could have died, she thought, to have done that sweet lady any service. She turned down a quiet street to give way unnoticed to a burst of tears.

It was not till she got home that she opened her parcel. She found a plain but handsome Church Service with her name written within, and the sentence, "Given to her by her affectionate and sincere friend, E. Clair." It was enclosed in a case of coloured leather, and was just the convenient size to carry in her hand to church.

Patty had never seen anything so beautiful, and only wondered that Christian was not in better spirits, considering she had just come into possession of such a gift !

She had not forgotten to take Mrs. Clair's message to Kate Harley, about the duty of *waiting.*

"So you are to work, and I am to wait," said poor Kate, with a sigh. "You have the pleasantest task of the two, Christian."

Christian thought so, but she wished to reconcile Kate to what Mrs. Clair had said was evidently her duty.

"Mrs. Clair said, Kate, that either working or waiting was equally acceptable to God, if done to please Him, and she thought work would come to you in time."

"I will try and not be impatient, Christian. I

will do my best to *wait*. I am to go to father's farm
in the summer, and perhaps I shall come home as well
as ever." And then the two girls chatted on other
subjects so merrily, that it did Mrs. Harley's heart
good to hear her child's cheerful laugh, and she said
to her husband that she believed Christian would turn
out the best doctor for Kate after all. None of the
London ones had done half as much for her. And in
the fulness of her heart the good woman put a nice
new milk cheese covered with green rushes, into
Christian's hand, as she passed through the shop on
her way out, and told her to accept it as a present
from Kate.

CHAPTER XI.

"———— No sin, no grief, no pain,
Safe in my happy home !"

ALTHOUGH her daily visits to the infirmary took up a good deal of her time, Christian had not neglected poor little Tom, who was getting thinner and weaker day by day. She had taken him more oranges, and since Mrs. Clair had given her the sovereign, she had ventured, with Mrs. Harley's approbation, to buy him some grapes, for they were the only things he cared to touch. Nelly would not leave his bedside for a moment. She could not read, but she had a sweet voice, and Christian had taught her some verses of different hymns to sing to him. He liked her to go over them again and again, and Nelly never wearied so long as she was soothing Tom.

One afternoon Christian met the parish doctor just

8

coming out of the house.   She moved aside to let him pass, and he stopped an instant.

" You are the little girl who brings that poor boy grapes, I see," and his eye glanced at a small bunch she was carrying in a basket.

" Yes, sir, I bring them, but a lady has given me money to buy them for him."

" They have been a great help to the poor child, whose illness has been of a kind to keep him constantly parched with thirst ; but he will not need many more."

" Is he much worse, sir ?"

" No, not much.   He has been dying very gradually for some time, and the end is drawing near now."

Christian felt full of awe at these words ; the approach of death made her tremble.   But there was nothing to alarm her in Tom's appearance.   He was lying on the larger bed now, propped up high because his breathing was difficult.   His mother was stitching at some work which had to be finished, for the poor must work in the midst of trouble !   On the bed by his side sat little Nelly, who was just beginning to sing.   Tom's eyes were closed, but merely from exhaustion, for he was not sleeping.   He did not hear or see Christian enter, so she made a sign to the child to go on. Then she sang :—

"I close my heavy eye—
  Saviour ever near!
I lift my soul on high
  Thro' the darkness drear.
Be Thou my light, I cry,
  Saviour ever dear!

"And when I come to die—
  Saviour ever near,
Receive my parting sigh,
  And in the hour of fear
Be to my spirit nigh,
  Saviour ever dear!"

There was a pause when her voice ceased. It seemed almost as if Tom must be asleep, he lay so still; but in a few minutes, without opening his eyes, he gently pressed Nelly's hand, which lay in his, a movement which she knew meant that she was to sing again.

Then she began :—

"Sun of my soul, Thou Saviour dear,
  It is not night, if Thou be near;
Oh, may no earthborn cloud arise,
  To hide Thee from Thy servant's eyes.

"When the soft dews of kindly sleep,
My wearied eyelids gently steep,
Be my last thought, how sweet to rest
For ever on my Saviour's breast."

She did not know any more of the verses, Christian having only taught her those two. There was another pause, and then Tom opened his eyes, and for the first time saw Christian.

"Oh, I am glad you are come," he said; "I have been watching for you all day. Please read to me about Jesus."

Then Christian opened the Testament, and read till he grew restless, and asked for his mother to give him some water. He could not eat any grapes to-day.

"I wish Nelly could read," he said, when a little refreshed. "Mother, how can Nelly learn?"

His mother did not know; how should she, poor soul, scarcely able as she was to earn enough to keep soul and body together! But she said—

"We will try to manage it somehow, dear."

"I want her to be able to read about Jesus," he repeated.

"I think I know how Nelly may learn," said Christian. "I am sure it can be managed, Tom."

" Please be kind to her, when I am gone," he said. " She will be all alone when mother is out at work."

Nelly's lip quivered, as it always did when Tom spoke of going, and she drew closer to him.

" You will come, mother, and Nelly and Christian. We shall all be there some day, and Jesus will be there too."

He spoke in a low, wandering sort of voice, with his eyes closed; in another minute he had fallen into a slumber.

" He will sleep some time now," said his mother. "Poor lamb, he is tired out; I don't think he'll last long."

Nelly was nestling almost in his arms before, she drew closer still as her mother spoke. Christian crept gently away, opening and shutting the door with noiseless touch. Early the next day, she was sitting at work in the little parlour, Patty was busy in the kitchen, when the latter heard a tap at the door, so slight that at first she thought she was mistaken, but it was repeated several times, and as though small hands were beating against it. On opening she found little Nelly standing outside, without a bonnet, crying piteously.

Patty knew her directly, for she had been there several times before.

"I want Christian," she sobbed. "Where is she?"

Patty took her to the door of the work-room. The moment she saw Christian she flew to her side.

"Tom is gone!" she said. "He cannot speak to me or hold my hand any more. Mother says he is dead."

Christian's tears fell with the child's. She gathered from her that he had never thoroughly awoke from the sleep he had fallen into when she was there. Once or twice he had opened his eyes, but had not spoken, and had fallen off to sleep again. Towards morning his mother, and a neighbour who was sitting up with her, saw a change come over him. Nelly was asleep, but they aroused her, that she might kiss him once more, for they saw he was passing away. It was like an infant dropping to sleep—a few gentle breaths, then a sigh, and Tom had left his home of poverty for ever; had gone to Jesus, in whom he had trusted.

It was some time before Nelly comprehended or believed that this was a sleep from which he would not awaken; that he had really escaped. But she saw the truth when she found that his hand fell powerless from hers, instead of closing over the fingers as before.

They wanted to take her into the neighbour's room

whilst they did what was needful for the little body, but she begged so hard not to go, that they let her stay. In the morning she ran off of her own accord to tell Christian, who soothed and comforted her in the best way, by telling her of Tom's happiness now; of his freedom from pain and thirst; and by giving her hope of meeting him again at a future time.

Patty took back the child lest her mother should be uneasy. Christian had to go to the infirmary, but as she returned she went to the room of mourning. She felt half afraid to open the door as usual. Twice she raised her hand to the latch, and twice withdrew it. She had never seen death, and she felt afraid of this first view of him. At last she gained courage and entered. It was no terrible sight met her eye. All was orderly in the room, much more so than usual. A coarse but clean sheet served as a coverlid to the little fair corpse, whose features, always pleasing, were now calm and beautiful in their repose. Christian thought she could never tire of looking at them. The mother sat at the same work as on the previous days, there was no rest as yet for her. Nelly sat on the foot of the bed, she liked that place best. On a plate lay the untasted grapes brought the day before. Miss Bonar had advised Christian that morning to give the poor woman a few shillings of Mrs. Clair's money. She did so, explaining how it had been given into her keeping. The gratitude with which the much-needed help was received proved it was well bestowed.

A day or two afterwards Tom was buried in the nearest cemetery in the humblest manner. A child pauper's funeral! No event is looked on with less interest by the hurrying passers-by, who would stand still to gaze with curiosity on the white trappings of the rich man's child when carried to its grave. Yet what matter to little Tom, that only his mother, and Nelly, and one neighbour followed his coffin. *He* was not there, but far away, where there are no distinctions such as earth holds important. He was where all are alike in the sight of Him who is gradually collecting his own around Him.

CHAPTER XII.

"Go forth into the country,
    Where gladsome sights and sounds
  Make the heart's pulses thrill and leap
    With fresher, quicker bounds."

A DAY or two after Tom had been laid in his grave, Christian went to Kate. She found her as usual in the little back-parlour, but she was beginning to look much stronger, and was able to get up earlier in the day, and go out for short walks. She was improving fast, but time often hung heavy on her hands.

"I'm so glad you've come, Christian. I thought you had forgotten me."

"I've had a good deal to do," replied Christian; "my aunt had some work for me to finish. And oh! Kate, poor Tom is dead!"

"Indeed!" exclaimed Kate, whose interest in him had been very great, although he was personally unknown to her. "Poor little Nelly! what will she do?"

" She is very unhappy ; I can't bear to see how she cries about him when I go there. I've something to say to you about her, Kate. I really think your waiting is over, and that there is work come for you, if you will take it."

" What do you mean ?" inquired Kate, in surprise.

" The last time I saw Tom, he said he wished Nelly could learn to read about Jesus, and he asked his mother how it could be managed. She said she would try, but I knew she was too poor to think of being able to do more than just to feed and clothe her. She can sometimes not even do that when she has no work. So I said I was sure I could get her taught, and then Tom looked happier."

" And do you mean to teach her yourself ?"

" I am afraid I should not have time for her as well as Patty and the workhouse, but that is the work I thought was perhaps come for you, Kate."

A flush of pleasure passed over Kate's face. " I never taught a child," she said, " but I suppose I could."

" Of course," said Christian ; " it only wants patience. Perhaps Nelly would be quicker than Patty. Oh, dear! it's hard work with *her* sometimes, but she's getting on."

"I must ask mother's leave," said Kate. "I am sure she will let me."

Mrs. Harley was both willing and glad when the girls told her of their plan. It would be useful employment, she thought, doing good to Nelly and Kate at the same time; and she promised to give the spelling-book and copy-books, and pens, too, if she liked to add writing as well.

"And when shall she begin?" asked Kate, who felt impatient for the first sight of her new pupil.

"Shall I bring her on Monday?" said Christian. "She may have got a little over her grief by that time." She did not tell them that another reason why she wanted to delay was, that she might be able to finish a black frock she was making for the child out of an old skirt of her aunt's, which she had allowed her to have for the purpose. She had managed to cut it out herself, and she had taken it to the infirmary to show Miss Bonar, who was really interesting herself in its progress. This was the work alluded to when she told Kate she had been busy.

Nelly was a pretty child, and Christian felt quite proud of her when she saw her dressed in her little black frock, with a piece of black ribbon tied round her hat.

A kind neighbour had lent her one of her children's black dresses to go to the funeral in, but of course it had to be taken off and returned afterwards. Nelly was very pleased to get one of her own, for she knew that sisters wore mourning for their brothers when they died, and she had not liked putting on her coloured frock again.

She was glad to be told she was to go and learn to read, and started with Christian on Monday, happier than she had been since Tom's death. Kate and she soon became acquainted with each other, for Kate had a pleasant, winning manner, and Nelly was not a shy child, but bright and intelligent. There was not much teaching went on in that first lesson, so called, nor in the second or the third, for Mrs. Harley, who dearly loved children, could not resist the temptation of bringing forth an old doll of Kate's, which so entranced Nelly, that it was in vain to try and think of A B C. But when at last the first novelty was wearing off, Kate thought it high time to begin in earnest, and the doll was put away, only to be reproduced as a reward for attention.

She came every day for a short time, and Kate liked the feeling that she was employing herself usefully. Finding that Nelly's stock of under-clothing was extremely limited, she thought she would begin and make her various articles. Mrs. Harley found materials, new and old, for the purpose; cut them out, and showed Kate how to do them; whilst, with her own motherly fingers, she cast on the stitches for a pair of socks, which she intended to be the first of several pairs for the little girl. Even Mr. Harley seemed to become inspired with an interest in the fair-haired, sable-clad child, whom his Kate seemed so fond of, and he gave her a new pair of boots, " on purpose," he said, " for her to trot backwards and forwards in every day." So Kate's work had come to her sooner than she expected.

The time arrived when it was thought safe for Miss Bonar to leave the infirmary. Patty was delighted to welcome her back, and took care to have her kitchen the perfection of neatness. It would have been difficult for even her mistress's keen eye to have found a speck of dirt about, or a thing out of its place.

Her health had sustained a considerable shock by her accident. The doctors advised her to go into the country, if possible, for a few weeks' change of air, an idea which she never really gave a serious thought to, hoping it would be unnecessary to leave home.

Mrs. Harley came to see her, bringing in her basket various little country gifts, such as a few new-laid eggs, some fresh butter, and a nice, plump little chicken. She gave it as her opinion, that the doctors were quite right about change of air.

"If you can manage to go, you had better," she said. "It will be cheapest in the end, for you'll not pick up your strength in this confined street, and you'll not be fit for much work till you are stronger."

When a week or two had passed, and still Miss Bonar felt languid and good for nothing, although her arm was nearly well, she began to think Mrs. Harley's advice was good, and that it might be as well to draw from her savings, which she could well afford to do for such a purpose.

But where to go? how to go? What to do with Patty and her house whilst she and Christian were absent? These were difficulties so formidable, that she saw no way of overcoming them.

"Christian," exclaimed Kate, one bright morning, "I'm going to the farm to stay some time. It's all settled, and mother has got such a plan in her head, all about you and your aunt, if only she will consent to it. There are some nice, cheap lodgings in a cottage near my brother's house, and if Miss Bonar would take them, she would get strong again, and you and I could be together all day long. I am to have a donkey, and so we should be able to go long walks, and sit in the hay-fields, and have all sorts of fun."

The thought of country walks and hay-fields made Christian glow all over, but it was hopeless to suppose her aunt would go.

"Mother is going to talk to her about it this evening," said Kate; "I do hope she will consent."

"Is it far away?"

"About twenty miles. The name of the village is Leafdell. There is a railway goes through it from London. Our butter and eggs, and things, come up by train every day. Do you think you can persuade Miss Bonar to go?"

"Your mother could, perhaps," said Christian; "she thinks so much of what she says always."

Mrs. Harley came in with a large bunch of flowers in her hand.

"These came up in the hamper to-day, Kate, and I forgot to bring them to you."

They were the sweet-smelling June flowers generally to be found in a farmhouse or cottage garden

—stocks, carnations, mignonette, rockets, sweet Williams, etc., etc. The little town room was filled instantly with their perfume. Kate buried her face in them for an instant, and then passed them over to Christian.

"You shall have half of them," said Kate, "to take home with you. Perhaps the sight of them will make Miss Bonar long to go to Leafdell."

"What does Christian think of our plan, Katie?"

"*She* would like it, mother; and she thinks you might persuade her aunt to go."

"I'll go over to her at once," said Mrs. Harley; "I'm not wanted in the shop just at present. I'll tell you what it is, Christian. If your aunt doesn't go somewhere soon, she'll be too poorly to be able to leave at all, and so I shall tell her."

She put on her bonnet and shawl, telling Christian to stay with Kate till her return. She came back in less than an hour, and, to the great delight of the girls, said that Miss Bonar had seemed quite pleased at the proposal, as she really felt the desirableness of change, but did not know where to go, or what it would cost; and what to do with her house and Patty was a difficulty.

"But we've settled it all," she said. "I told her the cost of the journey and the lodgings, and she says she can manage it; then as for the house and Patty, I've hit on a capital idea. Patty's old granny is to be asked to come and be with Patty. So it's all arranged."

For some minutes the talk was about the delights of Leafdell, and what they would do there. Then Nelly was remembered, and Mrs. Harley promised to give the child a lesson now and then, that she might at least not forget what she had learnt of her letters.

Christian's thought was about her old women. The fear that they would miss her reading was the only drawback to her enjoyment in the prospect of going to Leafdell.

She divided the flowers Kate gave her into several small nosegays the following day, and took them with her to give to the poor bodies who rarely saw a flower. Slight as was the gift, it delighted them more than one of greater value could have done. Christian could scarcely have touched their hearts more than by this simple action of love, and she secretly resolved that it should be repeated whenever it was in her power. There was universal regret when she told

9

them she was going away for a few weeks, all but from Molly and Betty, who rejoiced in her prospect of the country and fresh air.

"We can ill spare you, dearie, but it's right you should go and have your bit of pleasure," said Betty. "I'm right glad you are going."

"I shall feel quite idle there, I think," said Christian, "without having you to read to."

"You'll find something to do," said Betty. "Never fear that you need be idle. 'Tis not idleness to go into the fields, and look at the trees, and the grass, and the flowers by the hour together, if you think of Him who made them. When I was about your age," continued she, "I lived in a cottage down in the country. I didn't think much about the things around me, because I saw them every day, and had grown up amongst them. A tree was a tree, and a flower was a flower; I never thought once about how the tree or the flower grew, and what they had come from. But one day my mother told me to sit on a grass bank and watch my little baby sister, whom she had laid fast asleep on a shawl under the shade of a tree, for it was very hot weather. I got tired of my task, and complained I had nothing to amuse me; but mother insisted on my staying, as she was busy in the house, and did not dare leave the baby alone. There was an old man at work in the garden who used to be called 'Wise Roger,' because he was so fond of reading. He was a holy, good man too. When he heard me say that I had nothing to amuse me, he came to where I was, and plucking a dandelion, of which there were plenty about, he laid it on my lap. 'Nothing to do?' said he, 'pull that to bits, young one; take it carefully leaf from leaf, examine how it's made, how the flower grows on the stalk, and then think about the God who did it all, and how wonderful and great He must be: for there's no man who was ever born that could make a dandelion, though the doing it would save his life or give him all the riches of the earth.' He went back to his digging, but I took the dandelion, and looked at it with a deal of curiosity then; and the longer I looked, the more I wondered. I began to pick it carefully to bits, first one leaf, then another, till at last it lay in fifty pieces in my lap. I don't believe that till that moment I had ever thought about the great God being so wonderful and mighty as I did then. I examined a daisy next, and then a leaf with all the pretty little lines running about in it;

I had found plenty to do, and wished baby had slept on longer than she did, for I had to nurse her as soon as she awoke. But I never forgot about the dandelion, and all the thoughts it gave me. From that time I got into a sort of way, as it were, of examining flowers and such like things, and a deal of good it did me, for it always set me thinking about the Maker. So you needn't be idle, child," said the good old woman. "The fields and the gardens and the woods will be full of work for you, and they'll teach you many a lesson."

"Thank you, Betty," said Christian; "I shall pull a dandelion to pieces too; how clever it was of Roger to tell you to do it. They might well call him 'Wise Roger.' What became of him ?"

"He died, dearie, that is what must become of us all! 'Tis more than seventy years ago since he brought me the dandelion, but I can see him now as plain as I did then."

"Seventy years," exclaimed Christian, "what a long time that sounds! I wonder you have not forgotten everything that happened so far back."

"It is but as one year to look back to," said Betty; "and I seem to remember about things then, better than later on in life. I can't remember any place so well as the village where I was born, and I never saw any I loved half so much. I've lived in London all my life since."

"Have you ever been there since you were a girl?" asked Christian.

"Yes, dearie, I often went whilst my parents lived. I was put to service to a gentleman's family near, and then they went to live in town, and I with them. My mother died when I was about twenty-four, and there was only my father and sister left—she scarcely grown up. I wanted her to come to town and live somewhere near me in service. My mistress offered to get her a place, but she was a sadly spoilt girl, and would not hear of it. She said she must stay and keep father's house, and he petted her, and did not insist on her going, though he used to say afterwards he feared then she was scarcely fit to be trusted alone so much whilst he was out at work."

"And what became of her?" asked Christian.

"That's a question God only can answer, but I'll tell you all I know. She had been the merriest wildest little girl any one ever saw. She could not bear being in the house, but was fond of running about the woods, and could climb a tree like any boy. Mother always kept saying she would grow tamer when she was older, but she did not. Open air and freedom—that seemed to be all she cared for, even when she was no longer a child. Her greatest delight was when in the summer whole camps of gipsies came and pitched their tents near our village. Rachel used to get acquainted with them, and she would spend hours playing with their children, and amusing herself in some way or other about the tents. They led just the life she would have liked to lead herself. As long as mother lived she kept an eye over her, but when she was gone there was no one to control her, but she took care to keep father comfortable; with all her wildness, she would never neglect him. And if he found his meals tidily put on the table, and Rachel with her bonnie bright face ready to take them with him, he didn't trouble himself much about her, thinking all was right.

"Well, 'tis a long story, and now comes a sad part. A tribe of gipsies arrived from foreign parts, and stopped in a lane near the village. They were from Spain, some of them, and had far brighter black eyes and better looks than most of our own people. And

there was one young man who took a fancy to Rachel,
and she to him. Father knew nothing about it at
first, but when Rachel told him that they liked each
other and wanted to marry, he was furious. He said
no child of his should marry a tramping gipsy and a
foreigner, he would rather see her in her grave ten
times over. At first she tried coaxing, and said she
had always wanted to go and see other lands, and how
she should like a gipsy's life; but all that only made
matters worse. The neighbours backed father. They
said our family had always been so respectable, and
that such a thing was never heard of as any decent
girl going off with a gipsy lot.

"The end of it all was that father settled she
should go and stay with our aunt a long way off, and
not come back till the summer was over. He said he'd
take her himself. There were no railways in those
days, but they were to travel by a coach which passed
early in the morning. Rachel seemed content to go;
but when the morning came, it was found she had
gone off with her lover, and all we heard of her afterwards was from the clergyman at Southampton, who
married her, and promised, he said, to write and tell
father that he had done so, and that she was gone to

Spain, and would write from there. But we never heard of her again from that time except once."

"Then the gipsies did not come to your village any more?" said Christian.

"Never that Spanish set that I know of; others used to camp there, and I dare say do still, for Leafdell was always a favourite place with them."

"Leafdell! why that is the very place I am going to," exclaimed Christian.

"Dearie me, dearie me," said the old woman, getting quite excited for the moment. "Then you'll come and tell me how it looks, though it will be all altered now. But I'm glad you're going there; perhaps you'll bring me up a flower from the old place. There's a lane there called 'Vicar's Lane,' where I used to go with Rachel when she was a little one. I'd rather have a flower from there than from the finest hothouse in the world."

Christian promised, and felt more than ever anxious to go to Leafdell, now that old Betty's story had given the place such an interest.

CHAPTER XIII.

"There's a sweetness, there's a sadness
In the thought of days gone by."

THE railway journey to Leafdell, though it would have
been considered a trifle by people who were in the
habit of travelling, was a formidable affair to Miss
Bonar, who scarcely ever went from home. Kate
Harley had gone a week before them to her brother's
house, and wrote to Christian that the lodgings were
taken, and everything would be ready when they
came.

It was a beautiful July evening when they arrived
at Leafdell, and as they walked up from the station,
Christian thought that surely nothing on earth could
be more beautiful than the scenery around, and she
did not wonder that Betty Banks still retained such a
vivid recollection and love for it. The farmer, Mr.
James Harley, had sent a boy and wheelbarrow for

their boxes—Mrs. Harley having begged her son and daughter-in-law to show them any attention in their power.

When they arrived at their lodgings, they found they were in a small but pretty cottage, with a garden in front and behind it; the former filled with the gayest flowers.

Tea was set ready for them, with nice cream and bread and butter—all a present from the farm, to start them in their country housekeeping.

And soon came Kate, looking better already, and in higher spirits than Christian had ever seen her. With her was her sister-in-law, a pleasant, active little woman, who bade them welcome to Leafdell in such a kind manner, that she won their hearts directly. She invited Christian to come and see the cows milked, the pigs fed, and all the other farm sights, and told Miss Bonar there was a nice shady arbour in their garden, where she hoped she would come and sit whenever she felt inclined.

Very pleasant days followed. Miss Bonar grew stronger daily. Time might have hung heavy on her hands, if it were not that she found she could have as much employment as she chose in the dressmaking way, for Mrs. James Harley was glad to avail herself of her services, and it really did her more good to work than to be idle.

Christian and Kate, with their donkey, rambled far and near, for her aunt made it an entire holiday to Christian. Miss Bonar's sympathies had been wonderfully drawn forth by the kindness shown to her by others lately; and one proof of it was that she really delighted in seeing Christian's great enjoyment of this country life.

One day, as the two girls were returning home down a shady lane, they came suddenly on an encampment of gipsies, which had arrived a day or two before. It was no uncommon sight at Leafdell, but to Christian it was one of great novelty and interest; the more so because of the story Betty Banks had told her about her gipsy sister of days gone by.

Neither she nor Kate had any childish fears about gipsies. Those that frequented Leafdell were always, for the most part, of a peaceable sort, living by their own industry, and less given to pillaging the farmers' yards than gipsies are said to be wont to do; so they bore by no means a bad character in the neighbourhood.

A little girl with a brown skin, and eyes like diamonds for brightness, and sloes for blackness, ran out of one of the tents, and offered a prettily-made basket for sale. Kate bought it, and they chatted with the little creature as she ran by the side of her donkey, till, when they came close to the village, she left them, skipping back to the tents with fawn-like grace and speed.

She often met them in their walks afterwards. Her name was "Lizza," she said; she was about nine years old. She could plait straw, and make baskets, and her mother had taught her to read, and even to write a little.

The girls grew fond of her, and she of them. Sometimes she got them into the tent occupied by her father and mother and an old grandmother, who seemed very poorly. She was a tidy-looking body, but almost blind, and her head and hands shook with palsy. Her daughter, who was Lizza's mother, seemed very attentive to her, and all the camp treated her with respect.

Christian felt more at home with an old woman than did Kate. She reminded her of her friends at the workhouse, and she wondered whether she would care about being read to as they did. She thought it must be tedious work, hour after hour, doing nothing but knitting a little sometimes—oftener sitting listless, and being evidently ill.

She asked Lizza if she ever read to her grandmother; but it seemed to be a new and strange idea to the child, whose reading was at best nothing to boast of. She said granny asked her mother to read now and then out of a book she always kept near her, and which she never liked any one to touch without her leave.

One very sultry evening Kate and Christian passed the tents when granny was sitting outside. Her daughter had made her comfortable, and was gone into the wood close by to gather sticks.

They went up to her to bid her good evening, but she seemed low and out of sorts, tears were running down her cheeks, though she did not appear to be in great distress.

"Granny's always wrong when the bells ring," whispered Lizza; "she likes them, but cries like that."

The village bells were ringing a peal, according to an old custom, on Saturday night.

Christian's loving little heart could not bear to see

the old lady unhappy, and she stole up to her and ventured to stroke her withered hand as it hung down by her side.

"I am afraid you are not well;" said she, " I wish I could do anything for you."

"I'm not worse than usual," said she; "but my heart's sore—very sore and sad. I like to hear the bells ring, yet I would they would cease."

"Do you not like bells?" asked Christian.

"I used to like them years and years ago; but now I hear strange voices in them, and they mind me of my youth, and I feel the tears come as soon as they ring; and so, perhaps, will you, little one, some day, when you grow old like me—old and nigh to death," she added, softly.

Christian was puzzled what to say next. She wondered if the old woman was frightened at being "nigh to death." Tom had not been; but then he loved God.

At last she said, "Do you like to be read to? do you know about the Bible?"

She drew a small shabby book from her pocket.

"I've got one, and it's been a deal of comfort to me; read me a verse or two."

'She stole up to her, and ventured to stroke
her withered hand.' *Page* 142

Then Christian read a short psalm, and was closing the book, when her eye fell on a name written in faded ink in the title-page : " Rachel Banks, from **her** mother."

In an instant it flashed upon Christian's mind that perhaps this old woman was no other than Betty Banks' sister, who had run away from home.

" Please, was your name Rachel Banks ?" she said ; " I ask because that name is written in your Bible."

" My name *was* Rachel Banks once."

" And had you a sister called Betty Banks ?"

" I had a sister Betsey ; why do you ask ?"

" Because I think I know her very well."

" But they tell me no one lives here of the name of Banks," said she, much agitated.

" No ; she is near London, and I go to read the Bible to her as she lies in bed ; and she told me about a sister she had who was named Rachel, and that her home was once at Leafdell."

" 'Tis herself !" said the old woman ; " and she is still alive ! I thought she'd been dead for many a long year, for I got no letters from her."

Then she told Christian how she had received her sister's letter telling her of her father's death ; and that she had written several times after, but never got a reply ; so at last she concluded she too had died.

She had been in Spain all these years, leading a wandering life for the most part. She had lost several children, and this daughter alone was left her. Her husband had died several years ago: Her daughter had been her last-born child. It had often been her wish to revisit her native place ; but the tribe to which she belonged never came during all these years till now. Partly, to please her, they had turned their faces towards Leafdell to encamp for a time when they had arrived in England, where all places were pretty much alike to them. But the old lady had been much shaken by the journey, and was dejected at finding how greatly everything was changed, and that there was scarcely a person left she had known as a child. The bells alone remained the same, and they were more pain than pleasure to her now.

Many a question she asked Christian about her sister Betsey. Christian did not know any more of her history than its general outline, which was that she had lived in service for some years, and then had set up a small shop, in partnership with a fellow-servant, a respectable woman, who, like herself, had some money.

All went on well for many years, and Betsey had saved a comfortable sum for old age, when the bank broke, and she and her partner—who was no other than Molly Parsons—were left beggars. The workhouse had to become the home of both.

It was a strange link in the chain of events that had brought Christian from the bedside of one aged sister to another—the two being under such different circumstances. But it was God's will that the little girl should find a mission of love in the incident, for she was thus enabled to be a comfort to both, by taking news of each to the other.

For several days she used to go regularly to see Rachel, and read to her out of the little Bible which she had so carefully preserved during her wandering life all these years, a fact which was afterwards an unspeakable comfort to Betty.

When good Mrs. Harley came down to Leafdell to stay from Saturday to Monday, and heard the almost romantic tale of the sisters from Christian, her kind heart began to think whether it might not be contrived to get Rachel as far as Kensington, that they might meet once more in this world. But her scheme was frustrated by the sudden death of Rachel, who had a stroke and never rallied from it. Thus, after a strange, and, for an English peasant-born woman, a most unusual life, Rachel Banks had wandered back to Leafdell with the same gipsy tribe who had lured her from it about sixty years before, and was buried in the church-yard by the side of her parents. Her story had been almost forgotten in the village. Two generations had sprung up since the day when her disappearance had caused such a sensation. Only a few very old people remembered her as a wild, high-spirited girl, whom all liked, but who could never be tamed into quiet domestic ways.

Almost immediately after her funeral the gipsies prepared to leave the neighbourhood. The day they went away Lizza appeared at Miss Bonar's door, and asked for Christian. She brought her granny's Bible in her hand, which her mother wished to be given to Betty. Her mother was waiting near, she said.

Christian went to her, for she would not come in. She was a civil sort of person, speaking a mixture of Spanish and English, although she had married a man who was English by birth.

She said she should wish her aunt to have the

Bible, as she had heard her mother say she intended sending it to her, though she owned she was sorry Lizza should not have a Bible, as the child would not be in the way of hearing much about religion in their wandering life.

"She *shall* have one," exclaimed Christian, and she ran into the house and brought out her own, which she had used ever since she could read. She had another at home, given to her as a prize at school, and she thought Lizza ought to have one of the two.

So with many thanks Lizza took the book. Her mother said they should not be long in England; they meant to return to Spain before cold weather set in.

Christian kissed little black-eyed Lizza.

"You will read my Bible sometimes, Lizza, will you not?" said she.

"She shall," said her mother, speaking for her. "I've never cared for it myself, but perhaps it would be well if I began to do so. At all events, Lizza will, I hope."

They parted, and were never heard of more in England. But when Christian returned from her walk with Kate that afternoon, she found a pretty basket standing on the table, which their landlady said had been left for her by the little black-eyed child as a present.

Christian treasured her basket, and let us hope that Lizza treasured her Bible; and that amidst the wandering, perhaps almost heathen life she led, it shed its precious rays of light over the darkness with which she was surrounded.

CHAPTER XIV.

"Be our coming strength devoted
But to works of daily good,
Our brethren or ourselves promoted,
Homeward on the narrow road."

HOLIDAYS must come to an end, and so Miss Bonar and
Christian had to bid good-bye to beautiful Leafdell
and all its pleasant remembrances, very soon after the
gipsies left.

Kate remained behind with her brother and sister
for a few weeks longer, that she might get quite strong
before winter. However sorry Christian felt to leave,
she was impatient to see Betty Banks, and tell her
what would be so deeply interesting. She did not
forget to take with her some flowers from Vicar's
Lane, together with old Rachel's Bible.

We must not make our story too long, or we might
tell our readers all about the joyful greeting she received from the old folks the first day after her return.

How they clustered around her, and told that they had wearied for her to come back. How dear old Betty and Molly laid aside their knitting (for they were both able to knit) and gazed at her through their round tortoiseshell-cased spectacles with looks of love, whilst their lips spoke words of blessing, till Christian felt that not even the beautiful country scenes she had left, or her rambles amongst the sweet-scented fields and woods, had ever filled her heart with happiness such as it was experiencing now.

But uppermost in her thoughts was all she had to tell Betty about her meeting with her sister in the gipsy tent. For some time the old woman was quite incredulous. It seemed to her so wonderful and so impossible a thing, that the sister of whom she had heard nothing during a whole lifetime should have actually come back and died at Leafdell, she thought Christian must have made some great mistake. When, however, she produced the Bible, and pointed to the name in the beginning, Betty recognized it at once as written by her mother, and the strangely clear memory which old age retains for the things pertaining to its youth, enabled her to recall the very time and occasion on which it was given to Rachel.

"I remember it, I remember it," she exclaimed, her voice trembling with agitation. "It's the very same Bible as mother gave her on her fourteenth birthday! 'Twas always a comfort to my mind that she put it up to take away with her. She took nothing but that and a few clothes. And to think she kept it all these long years, and she a wandering gipsy!"

"Her daughter said she never could bear to have it away from her," said Christian; and she informed Betty of all she knew about Rachel's love for it, and how the sound of the bells had made her weep; she told her also of her sudden death, and her funeral.

Betty listened, and the tears stole down her wrinkled cheeks. At length she said—

"Truly, the Lord's ways are wonderful! Many and many a prayer have I prayed for Rachel, but never did I think to hear more of her on earth. Now I feel assured that I shall see her again. She couldn't have carried about her Bible, and loved it all these years, without having found in it the way to heaven, even if she'd forgot the teaching she had as a child. God be praised for all his mercies!"

She laid the precious little Bible by her side, and

then she looked at the flowers Christian had brought from Leafdell.

"It makes me feel young again," she said, " to look at them, and to know where they come from. To think how many a flower has grown in them lanes since I was a girl, and that at last some of them have found their way to me here !"

Christian had not forgotten to bring a little nosegay apiece for Molly and the other women, who were as pleased as children with them. To one and all they brought back pleasant memories of days gone by; and those who have watched over the declining years of the aged, know well how they love and cling to the recollections of youth.

When Mrs. Harley heard from Christian of the pleasure they gave, she told Kate and her sister to send some regularly thrice a week in the hamper, as long as there were any. So Christian rarely went empty-handed from that time till winter frosts set in, and flowers were few and far between.

Things began now to go on in their old course as before Miss Bonar's accident—that is to say, they did so outwardly. Work came in, and Christian had to sit at her sewing. Patty scrubbed and cleaned, and was as clumsy and affectionate as ever; but though life seemed the same, it was different, somehow, to both Patty and Christian: for a change more to be felt than expressed had come over Miss Bonar, who was far less irritable and hard to please than she used to be, though the old scolding habit still clung to her, for the ways of years cannot be suddenly laid aside, however much we may desire to do so.

But a greater change still was her interest in what interested Christian. However busy they might be with work, it was seldom, indeed, that she would allow it to prevent her from going to the workhouse. Once or twice, when, remembering Mrs. Clair's injunctions about never neglecting home duties, Christian proposed to stay at home in order to complete something which she knew was pressing, Miss Bonar objected to its interfering with her visit to the old women.

"It will be a pity to disappoint them. Leave the work, Christian; we'll get it done," was her remark on such occasions, instead of the grumble there once would have been given, and the order to sit still, for she couldn't be spared.

And one day, to Christian's surprise and pleasure, she proposed going with her to the workhouse.

At first she felt rather perplexed and shy when Christian lead her up to the women. But who could feel awkward long with two such loving old souls as Betty and Molly? They told her what a comfort her niece was to them, and they thanked her for allowing her to come, almost as though she were a benefactor to them for sparing the child.

Soon after this visit, Christian took the measles, and although she had them favourably, she was confined to the house for two or three weeks.

But even then the women were not left quite to themselves, for once in each week Miss Bonar might be seen, seated in Christian's place at the foot of the beds, reading God's Word aloud to her grateful listeners.

So great had been the power of that word on her own soul, that she could no longer go on living for herself alone.

Soon after Christian's return from Leafdell, she was made happy by receiving a letter from Mrs. Clair, who, after spending the summer months at a German bathing-place, was about to go to the south of France for the winter and part of the following spring. She said she had benefited greatly by the German baths, and hoped to return home in much stronger health the following year. She asked a great many questions about all those in whom she and Christian were interested, and she requested her to write her a full account of all that had happened to any of them since she left home.

Christian had never written but one letter in her life, and that was to Mrs. Gibson, in Australia. She felt it would be less easy to send one to such a lady as Mrs. Clair. How to tell her all she had to tell about Tom's death, and their going to Leafdell, and meeting with Betty's sister, and yet to write quite respectfully, rather perplexed her mind.

But Mrs. Harley, to whom she confided her trouble, soon settled the matter in her own blunt straightforward way.

"I'll tell you what you must do," she said; "just try and forget you are writing a letter, and let your pen put down the very words you would *say*, if you were talking to the lady in her own room, as you have done again and again. You were never once disrespectful, I'll be bound, even when your tongue talked the most."

The advice was simple and good; Christian acted on it, and found the letter was a much less formidable affair than she expected; she felt it very pleasant to fancy herself talking to the dear kind lady, whom she loved so dearly.

When the Leafdell leaves were beginning to put on their deepest autumn tints, Kate Harley returned to her own home, a very different girl in health and strength to what she had been before. She at once gladly renewed her reading lessons with little Nelly, which had been carried on by Christian in her absence, with her aunt's full approbation. But after Christmas the poor child lost her mother, and found herself left, as she had once so piteously expressed it, " All alone, and not able to die herself;" and again the cry arose from her lips "Oh, mother! oh, Tom !"

The workhouse could be her only home. She had not a relation able to befriend her. Mrs. Harley was interested in the child, and greatly desired to get her into an orphanage she had heard of, where she would be educated, clothed, and fed, and placed in a respectable situation when old enough to earn her own living. But at present there was no vacancy, and considerable interest was needful in obtaining a certain number of votes for the admission of a child.

Mrs. Clair would be all-powerful in procuring them amongst her extensive acquaintance, and would doubtless do what she could, but then she was abroad. Several other ladies, regular customers of Mrs. Harley's, expressed their willingness to exert themselves, but it might be some months at least before a vacancy arose, and it was contrary to the rules of the orphanage to receive a child from the workhouse. If, therefore, Nelly were taken there, even for a time, she would be considered ineligible to become a candidate for the next vacancy.

Mrs. Harley was perplexed. The orphanage would have been the making of the child, she said; she even asked her husband's leave to take her into their house for a time; but he, though a kind-hearted man, positively refused to give his consent to such an arrangement.

"Suppose, after all, they failed in getting her into the orphanage," he said, "they would not like to send her to the workhouse from their home; and to be burdened with her for the years that must pass before she could earn her own living, was not to be thought of for an instant."

Mrs. Harley owned the reasonableness of what he said, and with a sigh which came from the depths of her motherly heart, she saw that Kate's little intelligent, engaging pupil must go to the workhouse.

· That evening Miss Bonar made her appearance at Mrs. Harley's house. It was rather an unusual occurrence, although between her and Mrs. Harley a very kindly feeling, amounting almost to friendship, had sprung up. But greatly was the latter amazed when she found what was the object of her visit.

" I have been thinking," said she, " over poor little Nelly's case. It seems such a pity a child like that should go to the workhouse."

" It is a pity, indeed," replied Mrs. Harley ; " but there is no help for it."

" Yes there is," said Miss Bonar, " for I mean to give her a home myself, so long as there is no other she can be got into where she would be done better for."

" Do you mean you will take her into your own house, to live with you ?"

" Yes," replied Miss Bonar ; " the little she will eat will scarcely be felt by me, and she can sleep with ·

Patty, who will look after her whilst Christian and I are busy at work. As for her clothes, thanks to your Kate, she has a good stock of them. After a time perhaps she may be got into the orphanage."

"And suppose others get in before her till she is too old to be admitted by the rules," said Mrs. Harley; "have you thought well that such a thing is not unlikely? should you not feel you had undertaken a great charge? and would not the workhouse be a greater change to the child then than now?"

"Mrs. Harley," replied Miss Bonar, "I *have* thought well over everything, and still I wish to take this poor orphan into my own care till something better can be done for her; and if that something never comes, why then, God helping me, I'll do my best to bring her up, and put her in the way of helping herself."

"Well, I must say this is a thing I should never have expected," exclaimed Mrs. Harley; "but I'm as pleased as if Nelly were my own child, for she's a sweet, loving little creature. I wanted to do something of the sort for her myself, only my husband wouldn't hear of it, and so full of business as we are, ours isn't, perhaps, quite the house for her. Well,

Miss Bonar, it will always be a pleasant thought for you, that you've done two such good deeds in your life, for I've been told that you took your Christian from charity, when her parents died, because she'd no one else to care for her, and she not really your niece either."

"No, Mrs. Harley, I did not take her from charity," said Miss Bonar, a good deal agitated, "I took her from *pride*. I did not choose to have a relation of mine, even a distant one, in the workhouse; but for this feeling, I should not have cared what became of her. I've made myself believe for years that I deserved praise for what I had done for Christian, but when I lay on my bed in the infirmary, I learnt more of my own heart, and I knew then how I had been deceiving myself. I saw that I had been a proud, cold, selfish person; and when I read over and over again that chapter about the sheep and the goats, I trembled as I lay: for in taking Christian, I had *not* taken her for the Lord's sake, or for love; and had I been killed when I fell, I knew my part must have been with the goats, in everlasting punishment."

"You were hard on yourself," said Mrs. Harley, whose eyes were running over with sympathy, and whose tender heart would fain give a word of consolation, if possible.

"No, Mrs. Harley, I only could no longer deceive myself. Death came too close to me for that. But God has been very good. Instead of letting me be killed, He laid me on my bed for weeks, that I might learn to know myself, and with His help I will be different to what I have been. Nelly is cast on the world, and I look upon it that God is giving me the opportunity of doing something for *Him*, by taking her—at least for the present. For the future, I shall wait. He will show in time what it will be my duty to do with her."

Mrs. Harley said to her husband afterwards, that she should have liked to offer to share in the expense of keeping Nelly, but she really felt as if she dared not do it, lest it should be like trying to take from Miss Bonar part of what she saw she considered a great privilege.

Straight from Mrs. Harley, Miss Bonar went to poor little Nelly. Her mother had been buried, and she was crouching by a neighbour's fireside, heedless of the attempts of two children to get her to come and play with them. She knew she was to go to the workhouse next day, her chief comfort being that she had heard that Christian went there twice a week, and she might, therefore, hope to see her sometimes. Her curly head was leaning against the wall, and her pinafore was before her eyes, as Miss Bonar entered, and the plaintive cry still broke from her of—

"Oh, mother! oh, Tom!"

After a few whispered words to the neighbour, Miss Bonar gently took Nelly's hand, and told her to put on her hat and cape, for she was to go with her. At first the child looked puzzled and alarmed. She half thought this might be her summons to the work-house, but when Miss Bonar said she was going to take her home to Christian, her face lighted up with pleasure, and she trotted off fearlessly by her side.

Christian was not expecting her, for her aunt wished the arrival of the child to be a surprise. She knew how fond Christian was of her, and that she felt her a sort of charge, because Tom had begged her "to be kind to Nelly." She had no doubt of either Patty or herself being glad to receive her, even though a little trouble to both might be the consequence of her arrival. Perhaps the happiest moment of Miss

Bonar's life was that when she led Nelly into the work-room, and explained that she was to live with them, at all events till a better home offered.

When she felt Christian's lips pressed gratefully to her cheek, and and Nelly's little hand stealing into hers, as the child now, for the first time, clearly comprehended how matters stood, she felt that it is indeed more blessed to give than to receive.

As for Patty, her delight was so great at the novelty thus introduced into her life, that it took her several days to sober down into her usual ways; but if she spent rather more time than she ought in playing with Nelly, it had the effect of making the child so fond of her, that she was never any trouble to Miss Bonar or Christian, being always satisfied to be with Patty, helping or hindering her, as the case might be, whilst her daily instructions in reading, writing, etc., went on with Kate Harley as before.

Late in the spring, Mrs. Clair came home, so much improved in health that she no longer had to lie on the sofa as before, but was able to carry on many of her works of mercy in her own person.

Betty Banks had been failing the latter part of the winter. She lived just long enough to see Mrs. Clair once more, and to tell her with her own lips how great a comfort Christian had been. She gave Rachel's Bible to the little girl the day before she died. Her end was as her life had been, full of trust and hope in her Saviour.

Molly Parsons survived her only six months.

Mrs. Clair offered to get Nelly placed in the orphanage, but Miss Bonar wished to keep her altogether. The child had greatly endeared herself to her, and was getting on so well in every way that it was settled things should go on as they were. The last time we heard of her, she was acting as an attached and valuable servant to Miss Bonar in the place of Patty, who married a respectable young man in the shoemaking trade.

We must not continue our tale to greater length, or we might tell how, as Christian grew up, she continued to carry out the Scripture precept—

"To do good unto all."

Little loving acts, done in quiet unobtrusive ways, might be constantly traced to her, till in her humble sphere she acquired an influence over many, which mere wealth or position could not have given.

We have wished that other children should read the story of her early life, because we think it may encourage some who may have the wish to be useful, but imagine they are not so situated as to have it in their power. Perhaps they have not hitherto been looking about them to see if there is any old bed-ridden woman whose friends are too busy at work all day, and too tired at night, to read God's Word to her, which she often longs to hear. Or may there not be some child within reach, needing the clothing or teaching which its parents are too poor to give it. Would not even so small a present as a few flowers, gathered from the garden or conservatory, often carry with them refreshment and a sweetness greater even than their own to some poor invalid, because conveyed to them by the hand of kindness.

Think about it, dear children; and when you have thought, then try to *act*.

Remember that like the young heroine of the tale, *you* also have to prove yourself worthy of bearing the blessed name of " Christian."

BY THE SAME AUTHOR.

WORK FOR ALL; and other Tales. The Fourth Edition, in square 16mo, three Engravings, 2s. 6d., cloth.

These Tales have been written at the request of a friend who has much at heart the welfare of girls in the lower ranks of life. Their object is to show that wealth and position are not indispensable requisites to usefulness.

RICH AND POOR:

STORIES ILLUSTRATIVE OF RELATIVE DUTIES.

1   CECILE'S DISAPPOINTMENT.

2. WILLIE WINTON; OR, GOD WILL PROVIDE.

3. JANET'S YEAR WITH HER COUSINS.

4. MILDRED VERNON; OR, A LATE-LEARNT LESSON.

In small 8vo, Frontispiece, 3s. 6d., cloth.

WORKS FOR THE YOUNG.

COPSLEY ANNALS PRESERVED IN PROVERBS.

By the Author of "Village Missionaries," etc. Second Edition. With Six Illustrations, price 5s., cloth.

"A delightful book, and one which will afford pleasant entertainment to readers old and young. A thoroughly good and well-written story."—*Record.*

WAYSIDE PILLARS. By the Author of "Village Mis-

sionaries," etc. In crown 8vo, price 3s. 6d., cloth.

THE END OF LIFE, AND THE LIFE THAT HAS

NO ENDING. By the Author of "Copsley Annals." In crown 8vo, Frontispiece, 3s. 6d., cloth.

"This interesting little volume is well calculated to arrest the attention, rouse the conscience, and touch the heart."—*Record.*

"I MUST KEEP THE CHIMES GOING:" A Tale of

Real Life. By the Author of "Copsley Annals." Third Thousand. In large 16mo, Engravings, 2s. 6d., cloth.

"Patty Brooke is the daughter of a Norfolk labourer. We are introduced to her leaving the rectory-class on the Sunday before Christmas; and a few days after she goes to London, with a promise that she made the Rector's wife deep in her heart. She will keep the chimes going, 'Thanks be unto God for his unspeakable gift.' How she does this in the common rough work of a London lodging-house: how she cheers the poor sick girl in the two-pair attic: how she falls sick and recovers: and the chimes are kept going bravely all the time:—those who wish to learn will find in this charming, truthful little sketch."—*Christian Work.*

'BY MRS. MARSHALL.

VIOLET DOUGLAS; or, The Problems of Life. In crown 8vo, Frontispiece, 5s., cloth.

"Another charming tale; the narrative spirited, terse, and graphic; the tone pure and Christian."—*Church Sunday-school Magazine.*

THE OLD GATEWAY; or, The Story of Agatha. Crown 8vo, Frontispiece, 5s., cloth.

"The interest of this very agreeable book turns on the development of character. The inward world of the soul, with its ever-varying lights and shadows, is depicted with great skill and pathos. For this class of books Messrs. Seeley have established a speciality, and the present volume may be cordially recommended as in every way worthy of the healthy and instructive tales which have preceded it."—*Christian Advocate.*

MILLICENT LEGH: a Tale. In crown 8vo, with a Frontispiece, 5s., cloth.

"A sweet and pleasing story, told with a sustained and even grace."—*Guardian.*

HELEN'S DIARY; or, Thirty Years Ago. Second Edition, with Frontispiece, 5s., cloth.

"The style of the authoress is pleasing, and the interest well sustained. It has special attraction for the young, and can hardly be read without benefit."—*Record.*

BROTHERS AND SISTERS; or, True of Heart. Second Edition, with Frontispiece, 5s.

The hopes and fears of a large family in a cathedral city are drawn with much spirit. The dialogue is easy, and the tale above the average."—*Guardian.*

LESSONS OF LOVE; or, Aunt Bertha's Visit to the Elms. Frontispiece, 3s. 6d., cloth.

BROOK SILVERTONE, and the LOST LILIES: Two Tales. With Fourteen Engravings, 3s. 6d., cloth.

"We can heartily recommend this attractive little volume. The stories are genuine, life-like, and entertaining. The lessons are skilfully interwoven with the narrative."—*Record.*

*

BOOKS FOR THE YOUNG.

WHAT MAKES ME GROW; or, Walks and Talks with Amy Dudley. By the Author of "Harry Lawton's Adventures." With Twelve Illustrations by FROLICH. Price 3s. 6d., cloth elegant.

LITTLE ROSY'S VOYAGE OF DISCOVERY, undertaken in Company with her Cousin Charley. In large 8vo, with Forty-eight Illustrations by L. FROLICH. Price 6s. 6d., cloth.

"How children will enjoy this book! It is a story so natural in its conception, and so naturally told, that children will not ask if it is true, but will deem it a veracious book of travels."—*Standard*.

LITTLE ROSY'S TRAVELS; or, Country Scenes in the South of France. With Twenty-four Illustrations by L. FROLICH. Fourth Thousand, large 16mo, 6s., cloth.

"A thorough child's story, capitally told, and beautifully illustrated."—*Record*.

PETER LIPP; or, the Story of a Boy's Venture. Adapted from the French. Twenty-six Engravings on Wood. Crown 8vo, 5s., cloth.

"It is a simple tale, but its charm lies in the very pretty style in which it is told, and we may add, also, in the remarkable excellence of the illustrations with which it is plentifully adorned."—*Guardian*.

THE STORY OF A ROUND LOAF. Thirty-two Designs by E. FROMENT. In small 4to, 3s. 6d., cloth.

"The skill of an accomplished artist is shown in these graceful playthings of art; they are admirably drawn, and display feeling and taste. The story is happily told, and a pleasant book has been made."—*Art Journal*.

THE WARRINGTONS ABROAD; or, Twelve Months in Germany, Italy, and Egypt. Thirty-five Engravings, small 4to, 5s., cloth.

"A capital book, beautifully got up, and admirably illustrated. It is a marvel of cheapness, and yet will do credit to a drawing-room table."—*John Bull*.

HARRY LAWTON'S ADVENTURES; or, a Young Sailor's Wanderings in Strange Lands. Thirty-six Engravings, small 4to, 5s., cloth.

"A most attractive volume for young people. Such books at such prices are among the marvels of literature."—*Record*.

BOOKS FOR THE YOUNG.

AUNT ANNIE'S STORIES; or, the Birthdays at Gordon Manor. By the Author of "True Stories for Little People." In large 16mo, with Twelve Coloured, and Twenty Plain Illustrations, price 5s., cloth gilt.

Each of the Stories may be had separately, bound in cloth, gilt, with Two Coloured and Three Plain Illustrations. Price 1s.

1. LITTLE JOE AND HIS STRAWBERRY PLANT.
2. NORMAN AND ADA; OR, THE FIRST VISIT.
3. DONALD'S HAMPER.
4. THE BUNCH OF GRAPES.
5. LITTLE CHARLOTTE'S HOME IN BURMAH.
6. LITTLE NELLIE; OR, THE WAY TO BE HAPPY.

BROTHER BERTIE AND HIS FRIENDS IN THE FIELDS AND FLOWER-BEDS. By the Author of "Aunt Annie's Stories." In large 16mo, with Twelve Coloured, and Twenty-one Plain Illustrations. Price 5s., cloth.

LITTLE FRIENDS IN THE VILLAGE. A Story for Children. By the Author of "Aunt Annie's Stories." In large 16mo, with Twenty-three Illustrations. 3s. 6d., cloth.

GREAT THINGS DONE BY LITTLE PEOPLE. Large Type. Six Engravings. 2s. 6d.

WINGED THINGS. True Stories about Birds. In 16mo, Twelve Engravings. Large Type. 2s. 6d.

LITTLE ANIMALS DESCRIBED FOR LITTLE PEOPLE. In 16mo, Large Type, Eight Engravings. 2s. 6d.

TRUE STORIES FOR LITTLE PEOPLE. In 16mo, Large Type, with Ten Engravings. Price 2s. 6d., cloth.

BOOKS FOR CHILDREN.

In Large Type, with Engravings, price 2s. 6d., cloth.

"A series of books for little people, which does credit to its publishers."—*Guardian.*

THE WHALE'S STORY: Passages from the Life of a Leviathan. Large Type, with Six Engravings. 2s. 6d., cloth.

"A capital book for boys and girls. The clear type, the pictures, and the narratives abounding in anecdotes and stirring adventures, will make it a general favourite."—*Our Own Fireside.*

"This story will please the little folk—it is one that will keep a child awake beyond its bedtime."—*Standard.*

HORSES AND DONKEYS. By the Author of "The Dove." Large Type, Twelve Engravings. 2s. 6d., cloth.

GOOD DOGS; or, Stories of our Four-footed Friends, for Young Children. Large Type, Eight Engravings. 2s. 6d. cloth.

THE DOVE; and other Stories of Old. Large Type, Eight Engravings after Harrison Weir. 2s. 6d., cloth.

THE LITTLE FOX; or, Captain M'Clintock's Expedition described for the Young. Large Type, Four Engravings. 2s. 6d., cloth.

WAGGIE AND WATTIE; or, Nothing in Vain. By S. T. C. Four Engravings. 2s..6d., cloth.

THE LITTLE DOORKEEPER. By the Author of "Waggie and Wattie," "The Little Fox," etc. In large 16mo, with Engravings. 3s. 6d., cloth.

LITTLE LILLA; or, the Way to Be Happy. By E. C. Large Type, Four Engravings. 3s. 6d., cloth.